This month, in
LOCKED UP WITH A LAWMAN
by Laura Wright

Meet Clint Andover—a security expert who's
sworn off love. When the threats began,
he was determined to protect lovely
Tara Roberts—and watch over her night and day.
But in keeping Tara out of harm's way,
would he risk losing his heart?

**SILHOUETTE DESIRE
IS PROUD TO PRESENT THE**

Six wealthy Texas bachelors—all members of the
state's most exclusive club—must unravel the
mystery surrounding one tiny baby…and
discover true love in the process!

* * *

And don't miss
REMEMBERING ONE WILD NIGHT
by Kathie DeNosky
The third installment of the
Texas Cattleman's Club: The Stolen Baby series.

Available next month in Silhouette Desire!

Dear Reader,

Thanks for choosing Silhouette Desire, where we bring you the ultimate in powerful, passionate and provocative love stories. Our immensely popular series DYNASTIES: THE BARONES comes to a rollicking conclusion this month with Metsy Hingle's *Passionately Ever After*. But don't worry, another wonderful family saga is on the horizon. Come back next month when Barbara McCauley launches DYNASTIES: THE DANFORTHS. Full of Southern charm—and sultry scandals—this is a series not to be missed!

The wonderful Dixie Browning is back with an immersing tale in *Social Graces*. And Brenda Jackson treats readers to another unforgettable—and unbelievably hot!—hero in *Thorn's Challenge*. Kathie DeNosky continues her trilogy about hard-to-tame men with the fabulous *Lonetree Ranchers: Colt*.

Also this month is another exciting installment in the TEXAS CATTLEMAN'S CLUB: THE STOLEN BABY series. Laura Wright pens a powerful story with *Locked Up With a Lawman*—I think the title says it all. And welcome back author Susan Crosby who kicks off her brand-new series, BEHIND CLOSED DOORS, with the compelling *Christmas Bonus, Strings Attached*.

With wishes for a happy, healthy holiday season,

Melissa Jeglinski

Melissa Jeglinski
Senior Editor, Silhouette Desire

Please address questions and book requests to:
Silhouette Reader Service
U.S.: 3010 Walden Ave., P.O. Box 1325, Buffalo, NY 14269
Canadian: P.O. Box 609, Fort Erie, Ont. L2A 5X3

Locked Up
With a Lawman

LAURA WRIGHT

Silhouette®

Desire

Published by Silhouette Books

America's Publisher of Contemporary Romance

Special thanks and acknowledgment are given to Laura Wright for her contribution to the TEXAS CATTLEMAN'S CLUB series.

To the other Texas Cattleman's Club ladies, my new and wonderful friends: Sara Orwig, Kathie DeNosky, Cindy Gerard, Cathleen Galitz and Kristi Gold, five incredibly talented authors who took a new kid under their wing, showed her the ropes and gifted her with their amazing generosity.

And to my editor, Stephanie Maurer, who gave me the chance in the first place....

 SILHOUETTE BOOKS

ISBN 0-373-76553-3

LOCKED UP WITH A LAWMAN

Visit Silhouette at www.eHarlequin.com

Printed in U.S.A.

LAURA WRIGHT

has spent most of her life immersed in the worlds of acting, singing and competitive ballroom dancing. But when she started writing romance, she knew she'd found the true desire of her heart! Although born and raised in Minneapolis, Laura has also lived in New York City, Milwaukee and Columbus, Ohio. Currently, she is happy to have set down her bags and made Los Angeles her home. And a blissful home it is—one that she shares with her theatrical production manager husband, Daniel, and three spoiled dogs. During those few hours of downtime from her beloved writing, Laura enjoys going to art galleries and movies, cooking for her hubby, walking in the woods, lazing around lakes, puttering in the kitchen and frolicking with her animals. Laura would love to hear from you. You can write to her at P.O. Box 5811, Sherman Oaks, CA 91413 or e-mail her at laurawright@laurawright.com.

"What's Happening in Royal?"

NEWS FLASH, December—Deck the halls! Royal's very own Jane Doe is awake and out of the hospital at last! Only one problem—she's got amnesia. Jane is currently staying with nurse Tara Roberts while she recovers, but none of our reporters were able to slip past Cattleman's Club member Clint Andover to interview the woman, so we must continue to speculate....

Speaking of Clint, it seems that long, tall drink of Texan water has his hands full! More than jingle bells seem to be jangling Clint's nerves—Tara has him fit to be tied! Sources say that Tara and Clint were sweethearts in high school. Could that puppy love be blossoming into a full-blown affair? Everyone knows this particular bachelor was burned badly once—is he playing with fire again?

You'd better watch out.... Looks like all is not merry in Royal this holiday season! Rumors are circulating about mysterious letters containing dark accusations and deadly threats. So the question remains: Who is Jane Doe? Why did someone try to kidnap her baby? And what was she running from the night she collapsed in Royal Diner? This reporter hopes Jane regains her memories soon, because the young woman may be running out of time....

One

Clint Andover sat bolt upright in bed, his eyes wide, wild, his nude body dripping with sweat.

He swiped at his face, shook the sleep, the nightmare, from his muddled brain.

Three years of this. Had to be enough.

He glanced around. In the glass and steel bedroom of his five-story condo no fire blazed, no smoke hung. As usual, it had been a nightmare. Although, the massive burn scar on his chest would always serve as a reminder that it had not always been so.

Clint dragged a hand through his dark hair, listening to the sound of his heart pounding with fear—and sadly with life.

As it was every night, after the dream had come and gone, he didn't fall back against the mattress, didn't try to find sleep once again. He knew it was a lost cause. Instead, he ripped back his soaked sheets, stalked out of his room and down the hallway into his second-floor office, where the promise of solace awaited him.

The amber crystal liquid in the decanter on the bar winked at him.

The pale light from the predawn sky illuminated the large room, but Clint didn't need its guide. This was a nightly ritual.

He took a healthy swallow of whiskey, then walked over to his desk and dropped into a chair. Taking a look around, he snorted with derisive amusement. He was CEO of the largest security company in West Texas, had a room full of defense equipment at his fingertips—but ironically he couldn't use any of it to keep his mind from conjuring images of that night.

The night he'd lived.

The night he'd died.

Jaw tight, Clint drained the remaining liquid in his glass, then contemplated pouring another.

Wasn't it right that he be plagued with these nightmares? he mused petulantly. Wasn't it wise? Wouldn't these memories keep his soul locked away for good? Wasn't that what he deserved?

He gripped his chest, felt the bumpy, hideous flesh—felt the pain as his fingers dug a little too deeply.

No more whiskey. He needed coffee.

He had work to do. The work that kept him from just this, from thinking too much. He had the work of his friends to see to. The work of the Texas Cattleman's Club.

There was a woman with no name, no memory and a madman trying to get to her and her infant daughter. And Clint had vowed to guard and protect them both.

He stood up and faced the floor-to-ceiling windows.

Outside, the fiery dawn moved upward from the horizon at a steady pace. Just as it did every morning at this time....

Two

He was on the hospital floor.

And earlier than usual, Tara Roberts noted as she watched the new dark-haired OB/GYN stride into the elevator with the solemn frown he usually reserved for anyone who hadn't gone to medical school.

But this morning there was no one around to return Dr. Belden's curt appraisal with an apprehensive glance or a forced smile.

This morning the elevator was empty, and Tara felt the irresistible urge to take advantage of the situation, put aside her morning report and join him on his journey to the fourth floor. Whether it was improper or not, she had a few questions for the new doctor. Two questions that had been churning restively on her brain from the moment she'd been introduced to the man.

She wanted to know why she got a shiver up her spine whenever she caught his eye. But most important, she wanted to know just who he thought he was treating the nurses with such blatant disregard. After all, the nursing staff at Royal Hospital were some of the most caring and hardworking people she'd ever known, and it made her furious that she and her peers weren't given the respect they deserved.

But today she didn't get the chance to confront Dr. Belden. The door to the elevator closed too quickly on her silent queries.

On a restive sigh, Tara returned to her work. But as she stared at the report, her mind remained on the man. Granted, she wasn't a suspicious creature by nature, but the doctor just rubbed her the wrong way.

Maybe this newfound doubt had nothing to do with the new doctor and everything to do with the peculiarity surrounding her patient, Jane Doe. Actually, Jane Doe wasn't the woman's real name, but after waking up from a coma with no memory of who she was, the men of the Texas Cattleman's Club had christened her such and the name had stuck.

The Texas Cattleman's Club.

An altogether different type of shiver whispered through Tara as she pictured Royal's wealthiest, sexiest and most altruistic bunch.

Yearned after by women, respected by men, there

was nothing this group wouldn't do for the town of Royal and the people in it, old or new.

As they'd proved with Jane Doe.

Poor woman, Tara mused, grabbing another patient file from the board. Just a few weeks ago, Jane had stumbled into the Royal diner with her baby in her arms and a bag over her shoulder and had collapsed. Thankfully, several members of the club had been there. They'd quickly taken control of the situation and were now committed to helping Jane and her child.

Tara couldn't help admiring the men and their commitment. But that was all she would allow herself to feel for them. She wasn't about to get suckered in like the other women she knew, drooling over this one, mooning over that one. No siree. Her mother had instilled far too much sense in her for such ridiculousness.

"Life is for service," the old Irishwoman had advised her daughter all the way up until the day she'd died.

Life was for service, not for fun, flirtation or any other foolish—

"You aren't going to give me any trouble today are you, Tara?"

Tara pulled in a breath. Being startled was an unusual reaction for her. It was just that voice, that smooth baritone—it had always gotten under her skin, made her a little weak.

She hated that.

With a forced calm in her breathing, she turned

around and faced the owner of that voice. Walking toward her was Royal's foremost security CEO, a member of the famed TCC and one of the sexiest, most arresting men Tara had ever seen in her life.

He was also the first boy she'd ever kissed.

Clint Andover had certainly changed since junior high school. Sure, he'd been a cute kid back then, with killer blue eyes and a devastating grin. But today he was tall, dark and granite handsome. A man to be feared, a man women lusted over. Tara noticed that his mouth had turned hard, his frame unyielding and rippling with lean muscle. Clint Andover commanded attention from all. And those killer blue eyes? Today, they could make a lady's pulse pound an erratic rhythm if she looked into them for too long. And Tara couldn't seem to help herself this morning.

But there was more than just pulse-pounding sexuality in those eyes. There was also pain, sin and death living within this man.

And it was little wonder, she mused sadly, forcing calm into her blood. As most of Royal knew, Clint's past was not a happy one.

"Giving a man trouble," she said, her chin raised a fraction, falling easily into their usual morning banter. "That doesn't sound like me."

"Since when?"

"Since always."

"I don't think so." Clint stood rigidly beside the nurses' station, giving a quick nod to the unit clerk sitting behind the desk answering phones.

"Don't pretend to know me better than you do, Andover," she said lightly.

As he did with so many others, he pinned her where she stood with a dark, intense gaze. "My memory is exceptional, Tara. And I remember getting to know you pretty well."

She froze, feeling suddenly breathless. But there was no sensuality in his words, highly charged as they were. No, Clint was merely stating a fact, with no emotion at all.

Tara took a deep breath, tried to slow her rapid pulse. She would do well to adhere to the type of control Clint exhibited, she thought, the type of control she'd always prided herself on. But it wasn't any easy task. Around him she couldn't help herself. Around him she turned into a flesh-and-blood woman.

With memories of her own.

Memories of a young Clint Andover holding her close under the shelter of Royalty Park's beautiful gazebo, his father's aftershave tickling her nose as he covered her mouth with his.

"That was a hundred years ago," she said with a forced chuckle.

He took a step toward her. "Like I said, I have an exceptional memory. And you gave me trouble back then."

She stepped away from the nurses' station and lowered her voice. "An adolescent kiss is hardly trouble."

"It was for me," he said flatly.

Her throat dried up like cotton. Not because he

sounded as though he wanted to experience a little more of that particular brand of trouble, but because, God help her, she did.

They were taking their routine head butting to a foolish level. She needed to haul in the reins.

"Well, I'd say we've been getting on fine so far," she said tightly, "staying out of each other's way." She shrugged. "So, what seems to be the trouble now?"

"Yesterday you mentioned something about taking Jane out of the hospital."

Tara nodded. "She hates it here, Clint."

"She hates her situation."

"Yes, and it's being aggravated by being in the hospital."

"This is the best and safest place for her."

Tara frowned. "Safest? What in the world does that mean—"

He put up a hand to stop her, saying brusquely, "Nothing. I'm just suggesting if she needs further medical attention—"

"I *am* a nurse," she reminded him.

"Yes, I understand that. But bottom line? Jane is my responsibility and if I think she needs to remain here—"

"While she's on my floor, she's *my* responsibility," Tara interrupted, a little more sharply than she intended.

"Obstinacy is no virtue, Nurse Roberts."

"Neither is intimidation, Mr. Andover."

Nostrils flaring, Clint stared down at her and muttered, "Trouble."

Tara didn't move, didn't back down, even though the heat radiating off his strong, muscular body was almost unbearable. This word. This word he'd uttered with such severity. *Trouble.* She'd never been called such a thing in her life. And certainly not three times in succession.

She was strong willed, pragmatic and careful, yes. Those characteristics she embraced and relied upon.

But trouble? Never.

With anyone else, such an insult wouldn't be tolerated. But it was different with him. Why, she refused to even wonder about. But it was. When he looked at her that way, his body close, it wasn't such an insult.

When he looked at her like that, the word excited her as it slipped from his lips.

Frustrated at her unruly thoughts and feelings, Tara turned back to the desk, gathered up her charts. "I have work to do."

"So do I," he said.

"Then we'd both better get to it." She started to walk away. "Have a good day, Mr. Andover."

Clint grabbed her arm. "There's still this little matter of moving Jane Doe."

"I'm taking her home with me tomorrow," she said, agitation threading her tone.

"Dammit, Tara—"

"She's in excellent health. What she needs is a place

to relax and get her memory back. What she needs is to visit with Autumn. And I can take her.''

He stared stonily at her, arms crossed over his broad chest. ''David and Marissa can bring the child here.''

She ignored him, walked past him. ''I have patients.''

''You're not hearing me,'' he called after her.

''No, I'm not,'' she called back.

''Don't you dare move her, Tara.''

But Tara didn't acknowledge his command. She kept on walking, away from the man that had held her heart captive for too many years to count.

Her work, her patients, they were the most important thing in her life, and she would always do what was best for them even if it meant incurring the wrath of the daunting, dangerous and oh-so-desirable Clint Andover.

''She actually took her home!'' Clint shot his TCC buddies a stormy glance before dropping into one of the leather armchairs in the meeting room at the clubhouse. ''And after I gave her express instructions—''

Ryan Evans glanced up from his game of pool with David Sorrenson, and snorted. ''You gave a woman instructions?''

''Yes.''

''And you actually thought she'd comply?'' Alex Kent asked with a grin, pouring himself a brandy.

Clint frowned. ''I don't see the problem.''

''Take it from a happily married man who wants to

stay happy.'' David turned around, the late-afternoon sun blazing in from the windows behind him. ''*Never* give a woman instructions.''

Shaking his head, Ryan muttered, ''Happily and married in the same sentence. What happened to you, man?''

''Just wait, Evans,'' David retorted as he turned back to the table and quickly sent one of his solids into the right corner pocket. ''Your time's coming.''

''Not possible.'' And with that, Ryan missed his next shot.

David chuckled. ''Looks like your confidence is waning there, buddy.''

''You're such an ass,'' Ryan muttered, his dark eyes glinting with irritation.

''Can we get serious, gentlemen.'' Clint looked from one man to the other. ''I have a problem here.''

Alex dropped into the chair beside him. ''Does this nurse know about our attempted break-in?''

''To Jane's hospital room?''

Alex nodded.

''No.''

''What about the grab on Autumn?'' David asked.

Clint shook his head. ''She only knows what everyone else knows. The news reports of Jane collapsing at the diner and that Autumn is her child.''

David shrugged. ''Maybe you should tell her the rest.''

''I don't think that's a good idea.''

Alex nodded. "The less the people in Royal know about the dangers of this situation the better."

"I agree," Clint replied. "But without revealing that bit of information, I have little chance of getting Tara to take Jane back to the hospital."

"Well," Alex began, fiddling with his glass. "Looks like you might have to guard our Jane Doe from the nurse's house then."

A ripple of heat gripped Clint's chest at the thought of sharing space with Tara Roberts, but he brushed it off. Sure, he was attracted to the pretty blond nurse, had been since school, but this was business. And he never mixed business with pleasure. "Protecting Jane from Nurse Roberts's house?" Clint shook his head. "Easier said than done."

"Why's that?" Alex asked.

"Tara's a pretty stubborn—"

"Pretty and stubborn, huh?" David interrupted, his grin crooked. "Sounds interesting."

Clint shot his friend a dry glare. "It's nothing like that, Sorrenson. Tara and I are…well, we're just old friends."

Ryan lifted a brow. "No kidding."

"We've known each other since junior high."

"First brush with lust?"

When Clint didn't answer, just sneered, Ryan chuckled. "Sounds serious."

"How can it sound like anything?" Clint countered icily. "I didn't say a word?"

Pool cue in his right hand, Ryan pointed the cube of

blue chalk in his left at his friend. "That's why it sounds serious."

"We talking puppy love here, Andover?" David asked, grinning broadly.

Clint's chest tightened, and for a moment his mind blurred as the images of that night, of Emily, of fire and death, of all of it, threatened to choke him. He didn't want to hear words like *love* tossed in his direction ever again, and he made his position crystal clear as his voice turned low and menacing. "I've loved just one woman in my life."

The men sobered instantly. David and Ryan returned to their game, while Alex drained his brandy.

Coming to his feet, Clint paced the length of the Oriental rug. "There is nothing here and never will be. Tara and I are locked in a battle of wills, that's all. And it's about time I took control of the situation."

Alex nodded solemnly. "What do you plan to do?"

"Jane Doe can just as easily stay at my place as Tara's. Hell, they can both stay there if that's what they want. But our mystery woman will have my round-the-clock supervision, regardless."

"Just as long as you realize that you might have a fight on your hands," Ryan offered.

"Maybe so," Clint said, rising to his feet at the challenge. "But it's a fight I fully intend to win."

"Thanks, Tara."

Curled up on the couch in one of Tara's patchwork quilts, sipping jasmine tea spiked with honey, Jane smiled over at her. "I really appreciate this."

Tara returned her smile. "It's no problem."

"I don't know why, but that hospital felt like a prison."

"Some days it feels like that to me, too."

Jane stole a glance at the lovely fire crackling in the stone fireplace and sighed. "Your home is so cozy and comfortable and…"

"And what?" Tara asked gently when Jane paused.

The pretty, dark-haired woman shook her head, her violet eyes wistful.

"Closer to Autumn?" Tara pressed.

"Yes."

Tara gave her a sympathetic smile. Granted, she had no siblings, no children of her own to pine for, but every day that passed she missed her mother more. So, in some small way she understood Jane's melancholy attitude. "You must miss her terribly."

"I do. It's like a part of me is missing."

The wistful shades in Jane's eyes turned to moisture as tears welled up in their amethyst depths.

As she'd cared for Jane at the hospital, Tara had refrained from asking the woman too many questions about why Autumn was staying at the Sorrenson Ranch. It wasn't her business. But she couldn't help wondering. Sure, the hospital wasn't the ideal place for the baby, but it was close to Jane—far closer than the Sorrenson Ranch.

Perhaps as Jane grew to trust her more, she'd share

that information with her. For now Tara would just be a friend and an ear and a shoulder.

"I have the day off tomorrow," Tara said, leaning back in her overstuffed armchair. "How about we drive over to the Sorrensons' for a visit."

Jane's eyes lit up like two stars, and she nearly spilled her tea leaning forward. "Could we?"

"Of course."

"I would love that."

Coming to her feet, Tara gave the young woman a stern expression—one reserved for willful, but lovable patients. "Okay, but if you want some good energy to play with that child of yours, you'll need all the rest you can get."

A grin pulled at the corners of Jane's mouth. "That's nurse-speak for get up to your room and get some sleep, right?"

Tara laughed. "Right."

The doorbell chimed just as Tara was helping her guest from the couch.

"Expecting someone?" Jane asked.

Most of the people Tara knew were working at the hospital tonight. And she had very few friends. But there was someone who might have a bone to pick....

Tara grimaced. "I'm not sure, but I'm thinking a very nosy, very irritating man might be out there."

"Clint, right? The one who was guarding me at the hospital."

"That's the one."

Jane flashed a smile. "The tall, dark and very handsome bodyguard?"

An uneasy blush crept up Tara's neck as she muttered, "Well, I don't know about *very* handsome—"

The doorbell rang again.

"I am feeling pretty tired." Jane's eyes hummed with humor. "I'll be heading upstairs. And don't worry, I can make it to my room on my own."

Tara fought the urge to ask the woman to stay. "Are you sure?"

"Totally sure," she said brightly, turning to go.

Tara watched Jane climb the stairs, then walked toward the door mumbling to herself, "He's not all that handsome."

"Oh, who are you kidding?" Jane laughingly called from the landing, then promptly shut her bedroom door.

Tara rolled her eyes, then swung open the front door just as the bell chimed a third time.

His eyes as dark as the navy-blue sweater he wore, Clint Andover stood there, frowning. "So you are home."

"Yes."

"You cannot be trusted," he snapped, stalking inside her house without invitation.

"Well, hello to you to." She gazed at him in shock, stunned by his impudence yet intrigued by the spicy, woodsy scent of him.

"I don't appreciate having my orders challenged, Tara."

She followed him into the living room, trying not to take in his long, lean frame and tight backside. But it wasn't an easy task. "Well then, maybe you shouldn't be giving me any more."

"Tara—"

"I don't take orders from you, Clint Andover."

His back to her, he muttered, "Yes, that's exactly what they said."

She frowned. "Who said?"

"Never mind." He whirled to face her, the roaring fire at his back. "Tara, this is serious."

"I don't understand what the problem is. Why you're so worried." She shrugged, trying to read the impenetrable look in his eyes. "Jane is fine here, well taken care of."

"I'm afraid that nursing care is not enough."

"What are you talking about?" she asked, frustrated now.

"I'm talking about protection."

Tara stared at him. "Protection from what?"

His jaw tensed and he released a breath, but he said nothing. As he stood so tall, so imposing in the modest living room of her two-story house, he held something back, something major—she just knew it. But she also knew what a closed book he was. Probing him for answers wouldn't work.

Clint glanced at an old photograph of Tara and her mother in front of the Royal Public library on the coffee table, then found her gaze once again. "I've decided that Jane is going to stay with me."

Her eyes popped open. "Out of the question!"

"You can come as well."

She just stared at him as he attempted to rearrange her life with absolutely no assistance from her.

"Thanks for the offer, but we're staying here." She placed her hands on her hips, eyed him. "And unless you're prepared to get physical—"

His eyebrows raised slightly.

Tara faltered, then hurriedly stumbled along. "I mean, unless you're willing to pick me up and carry me over to—"

"Yes?"

The heat pulsing in her stomach dropped a few inches as his turbulent gaze bore down on her. "You know what I'm saying, Clint."

"Yes," he drawled, walking toward her, stopping within inches of her. "And luckily for both of us, physical force is not my style."

"Good to know," she said dryly.

He released a heavy sigh, shook his head. "You make me crazy, Tara."

Ditto, Andover. "Sorry about that."

"Fine," he said brusquely. "If you plan on keeping her here—"

"I do."

"Then understand that I'll be…around."

The word came out smooth as cream, and her heart flipped over. "Around?"

"Just get used to seeing my face, Tara." He left her

standing there, walked to the door, then paused. "And next time, you'll be *inviting* me inside."

Tara didn't move as she watched him leave. She refused to acknowledge the longing in her heart for one moment more.

Thankfully, when the door closed she felt as though she could breathe again.

Get used to seeing his face, she mused, dropping down on the couch, wrapping herself in the same quilt she'd loaned Jane some fifteen minutes earlier. How could she help it? She had seen, envisioned and imagined Clint Andover's gorgeous—and albeit a little daunting—face ever since junior high school. Good Lord, even the boy she'd dated in college had been judged against Clint and found wanting.

Even the one man she'd given herself to…

Tara closed her eyes and huddled deeper into the quilt, trying not to imagine Clint's kiss and the warmth that had flooded her belly all those years ago….

Get used to seeing my face.

No matter what it cost her, she had to fight this connection she felt for Clint Andover. He wasn't for her. Unless she could handle a brief affair.

A strange ache pulsated in her chest, then snaked lower.

And she wasn't altogether sure that she could.

She just had to keep her thoughts and desires buried for a little while. After all, Jane wouldn't be here forever. As soon as this mystery was solved, Jane would be back with her child, Clint would no longer be front and center and Tara could go back to a life of good sense and good service.

Three

Mother and child.

The beautiful sight of Jane cuddling her little baby girl, cooing and singing to her on the living room rug of David and Marissa Sorrenson's sprawling ranch as the scents of homemade pot roast wafted in the air, nearly brought tears to Tara's eyes.

Growing up an only child had made her yearn to care for others. And fortunately she'd found an answer to that calling in her work as a nurse. But even a sensible, safe, caregiver like her knew there was more out there for the taking. Family, children, a husband.

She just wasn't a taker.

Didn't know how to be, how to separate selfish desiring from simply deserving. But that wasn't all that held her back. She held on to an idea that the man in her life could turn into her father—abandoning his family, never looking back, leaving his wife and daughter to wonder what they had done to drive him away and into the arms of a different family. That scenario terrified her. It was too big a risk to take.

The future looked bright and safe the way she'd planned. And the wish for a family of her own would have to stay hidden in her heart.

Heck, she thought, handing a pink plushy teddy bear to Jane, she'd been hoarding dreams and wishes since junior high, since a certain sapphire-eyed boy took her in his arms and kissed her.

Tara's breath shuddered a bit as she recalled the way Clint had looked at her last night, how just his closeness, his scent, had turned her bones to butter.

A medical impossibility, of course. But that was how she'd felt. That was the memory she would add to the collection in her old woman's heart.

The baby's soft cries interrupted Tara's musings, and she turned her attention back to mother and child.

"Autumn is getting so big," she said with a smile.

Jane beamed at her daughter. "And so beautiful."

"She looks just like her mama."

"Thank you, Tara." The reply was soft, and Jane's gaze fell, not to her child but toward the floor.

Gently, Tara put a hand on her new friend's shoulder. "What is it?"

When Jane looked up again, anxiety and frustration

filled her eyes. "I wonder if she looks like her father at all."

Grief tore at Tara's heart. She couldn't even imagine what it was like to have no past, only the present and an unsure future.

"Don't worry," she assured Jane, giving her a quick hug. "It'll all come back. Just give it time."

"I hope so." With a melancholy smile, she eased Autumn into her lap and snuggled her close to her breast. "Memory is a strange thing."

"It is that."

Tara thought of her own memories. Some so cloudy, like geometry and gym class. And some so clear, like the scent of her mother's rosewater perfume, and the feel of Clint Andover's arms around her.

"Well, look who I found at the front door." Newlywed, Marissa Sorrenson practically danced into the living room, her brown eyes glinting, a smile curving her lips.

Tara didn't know Marissa all that well, but over the course of Jane's stay in the hospital they'd talked several times, and Tara had found the petite blonde to be a sincere and generous person.

A sincere and generous person with a gorgeous man beside her.

Tara watched Clint Andover walk into the room, his hooded eyes taking in the scene before him. Dressed in a black sweater and blue jeans, he looked incredibly handsome. His large frame seemed to eat up the space, just as his gaze seemed to devour Tara.

Or maybe that was just wishful thinking, she mused.

"Hello, Clint," Jane said warmly.

"Afternoon, Jane, Autumn." He nodded at Tara. "Nurse Roberts."

The dimple on Marissa's right cheek deepened. "Would you like to stay for supper, Clint? We have plenty."

"I'd love to," he said. "Just not tonight. Can I get a rain check?"

Marissa nodded. "Of course."

He gave her a tight smile. "I appreciate that."

"So, are you here to see David?"

His gaze moved to Tara. "Not exactly."

"Jane and Autumn, then?" Marissa asked, her tone threaded with amusement.

"Partly."

The look Marissa shot Tara's way had her wishing she could crawl right under the massive floor rug. But hiding was not at all her style, so she sat tall and proud and bravely met Clint's cool, blue gaze.

"I'm actually here to drive Jane and Tara home," Clint informed Marissa. "Since you gave them a ride over."

Tara frowned. "How did you know Marissa picked us up today?"

"Well, my first clue was that your car was in the driveway."

Jane giggled at this as Clint continued, "And the second was that David told me Marissa stopped by this morning to show you her new SUV." He tapped his temple, walked over to Tara and gave her a wry look. "Careful deductions…"

"Very clever," Marissa said with a smile.

"Yes, very clever," Tara agreed, flashing an indulgent smile of her own. "But we don't need a ride. Marissa is taking us back."

"Now she doesn't have to."

"But—"

"Give the newlyweds a break, Tara," he said, his voice smooth yet firm. "They need all the alone time they can get."

Tara bit her lip, though it wasn't really a tough decision. She didn't want to take away time from David and Marissa. But she didn't want to give in to Clint, either.

"Can I help you up?" Clint stood above her, his hand extended.

"All right."

As Clint helped Tara to her feet, Marissa and Jane not so covertly shifted their focus back to the baby. Tara had no doubt the women were playing coy, imagining that there was some kind of romance brewing between her and Clint. She'd have to set them straight later.

Once he had her on her feet, Clint eased her close and whispered, "I told you to expect having me around."

"But all the time?" she whispered back.

"Morning, night and everything in between," he whispered huskily. "If that's what it takes."

Heat swam in Tara's belly at his promise, but she forced a mask of composure. "You're so devoted to your work, Andover."

"You have no idea how devoted, Roberts." Something close to a grin, wicked and thunderous, flashed in Clint's eyes as he moved away from her, then said for all to hear, "Shall we go, ladies?"

It had been a long time since he'd driven a woman home.

Beyond the tinted windows of his truck, Clint watched the darkness of winter as it settled over the trees and land, turning them both a steely shade of gray.

In the back, Jane Doe rested comfortably against the leather seats, her eyes closed, her breathing even. She'd fallen asleep about five minutes after they'd passed through the iron gates of the TX S Ranch, leaving Clint and Tara free to talk.

But Tara had remained relatively quiet, every now and then humming along to the radio. She had a husky, soulful tone, very different from her regular speaking voice, and listening to her Clint couldn't help but wonder what other contradictions she possessed.

An up-tempo country song gave way to a soft ballad, and Tara once again began to hum. The growing darkness in the truck and the sound of her did something to him, went straight for the rogue that resided in him and hung on tight. And he knew that if he didn't watch it, he was going to give in to the irresistible urge he had to put his arm around her and pull her close to his side, like they were at some drive-in movie and not on a mission to protect Jane.

So, for tonight he chose words over action. "You have a nice voice, Tara."

She turned to him and smiled. "Thank you. Miss Ellis, twenty lessons."

He didn't try to hide his surprise. "You took voice lessons?"

"In tenth grade. No one knew. Not even my mother." She lowered her voice as though the woman was actually in the truck with them. "She wouldn't have approved of something so…"

"So?"

"Trivial, I guess. Frivolous." She sighed, leaned back against the seat. "You'll probably find this funny, but there was a time I thought about singing professionally, like in a jazz club. I wanted to be a torch singer."

"The blues?"

"Yeah."

"I don't think that's funny at all."

She shrugged. "Well, I was young…"

"We all have dreams when we're young," he said a little too tightly. "It's important."

Glancing over her shoulder at him, Tara asked, "What did you want to be when you were a kid? Policeman? Rodeo rider?"

Her query brought on a wave of memories. And for one brief moment Clint was twelve years old again, back in his grandmother's house. He was going through a box of his parents' things. They'd died just six months earlier in a car accident. He missed them desperately, and seeing, touching their belongings, their work, always seemed to make him feel closer to them.

Reading their work still had that effect on him. They had both been writers; his father a journalist, his mother, a novelist and poet.

"Too far back to remember?" Tara teased gently.

"Old man at thirty-five, huh?"

She laughed. "I didn't say it. You did."

"No," he said, turning off the highway. "I remember. When I was a kid, I thought about becoming a writer. Short stories, suspense, that kind of thing."

She didn't say anything for a moment, and Clint wondered if she was a little shocked by his revelation. After all, head of a security firm was a far cry from the romantic world of writing.

Finally he heard her sigh and say with just a touch of melancholy, "Looks like we both have an itch to explore our creative sides."

Clint ventured a glance in her direction. Outlined in moonlight, her curly blond hair falling about her shoulders, her lips parted and moist, she was something else. Try as he might to quell the desire that rushed through his body at a heady pace, just the sight of her sitting beside him in his truck made his chest tight, made him need and want things he shouldn't even be considering.

Sure, he had an itch to explore—*her*.

But he was on assignment, not on the hunt.

"I lost track of you after high school," she said suddenly, tugging him back to reality. "Where did you go?"

"To college, then into the military."

"The military?"

"Special ops."

"Very hush-hush, right?"

He cracked a smile. "Right."

"Military…wow, that explains so much."

"Like why I'm so rigid and serious?"

"And relentless," she added with a quick, bright smile in his direction.

"Well, when there's something I want, something that's important to me, I can't be stopped."

Tara felt her breath catch at his comment, and tried like anything to cover the sound. Her reactions to this man and his words and his eyes and his touch seemed to be intensifying every moment. It was as if she was no longer in control of her emotions and responses. She'd actually had to change the subject after he'd told her about his childhood interest in wanting to be a writer. The idea of the big, bold, dangerous, Clint Andover using his creative side had so surprised, so intrigued her she'd nearly ripped off her seat belt in order to move closer to him like some crazy teenager. It was ridiculous.

She was ridiculous.

"What about you, Tara?"

"Me?" she fairly stuttered, turning to face him. Which was a mistake.

His profile seemed cut, sculpted out of granite, in the shades of moonlight. She wondered what his jaw, his skin, would feel like against her mouth. Would it be the perfect combination of rough and smooth?

She swallowed hard. Would his lips feel the way she remembered? Cruel, hungry, almost punishing, even for a young man.

Forcing herself to look away, out the passenger-side window, Tara crossed her legs and took a deep breath. Were they close to home?

"What about you, Tara?" he asked again. "Where did you go after high school?"

"I stayed in town. I was going to go straight to college, but…"

"What happened?"

Pain squeezed her heart at the thought. "My mom got sick. Cancer."

"I'm sorry."

"Thanks." So was Tara, every day. The woman may have been strict and uncompromising in her beliefs, but she had loved her daughter with everything that was in her. "She wanted to go back to Ireland once more before…so, I took her." The heaviness in her chest lifted slightly as she remembered the wonderful time they'd shared. "Then, after she passed away, I started school."

"She'd be very proud of all that you've done."

"I think so. I hope so. You know, losing someone you love…there's nothing worse."

The interior of Clint's truck grew very quiet as the

weight of Tara's words sank into both of their souls. Trisha Yearwood crooned on the radio, and the sound of cars whizzing past them on the left as they rounded her street accompanied the singer. With all of her heart Tara wished she could take the words back, but it was too late. She hadn't been thinking about Clint's loss. She should have.

She peered over at him. He was staring straight ahead, his jaw as tight as his grip on the steering wheel. A flash of despair shot through her. He was still so torn up about his wife's death. And understandably so.

Through the rumor mill, the one that had only provided Clint's romantic history and not his educational endeavors to the ladies of Royal, Tara had learned that he'd been over the moon for his wife. He'd met her one night at Claire's in town, and they had married the next week. The thought of so much love flowing through this hard-edged man made Tara ache with want and admiration and just a little envy.

When they finally reached home and pulled into her driveway, Tara turned to wake Jane, but Clint stopped her.

"Don't disturb her. I'll take her up."

"All right."

Tara watched as Clint gently lifted the sleeping woman as though she weighed no more than a child and carried her into the house. Once again, envy moved through her, and a longing to be cared for in such a way, by such a man.

For one brief moment she allowed herself to imagine

what it would feel like to be carried to her bedroom in Clint Andover's arms.

Then her practical side gripped her mind, gave her a quick dressing down and reminded her of her place in life.

She collected the mail and the newspaper and followed Clint inside her house.

"She's staying in the upstairs bedroom," Tara whispered to him as she set her purse on the counter and held up what looked like her first Christmas card.

She didn't have loads of friends, but the few that she did have always sent cards around the holidays. The gesture made her feel less lonely, made her feel as though she still had some family.

But this was no holiday card, she quickly realized.

Confusion entered her blood first, followed by a blast of sheer black fright.

Again she scanned the thick, cream-colored paper. Then the matching envelope. There was no return address, and it had been mailed that very morning from Royal.

"What? Why?" Her pulse slamming in her blood, she shook her head. "I don't understand—"

"All tucked in," Clint announced, his movement light as he walked down the stairs. "I just took off her shoes and put a blanket over her, figured you could... Tara?" His eyes narrowed as he looked at her.

And it was little wonder. Tara could actually feel the paleness of her skin, hear the panic in her eyes.

Clint was at her side in seconds, his hand on her shoulder. "What is it?"

"I'm sorry, Clint."

"For what?"

She leaned back into his hand for warmth, for support. "You talked about protecting her. I didn't understand…" She shook her head, her words lost on the moment.

"What the hell are you talking about?" he demanded, staunch control setting his expression. "What's wrong, Tara?"

She held up the boldly typed letter. "This. It just came. It says that Jane is a thief and a liar." Her stomach clenched as she uttered the next words. "It says she stole little Autumn."

Four

"Can I take a look at that?"

Clint's query came out closer to a demand than a request, but Tara didn't take offense with his tone. She was too worried.

Lord, how long had it been since her hands had shaken like this? she wondered as she passed the letter to Clint. Probably back in those first weeks of nursing school. She'd been so afraid of making a mistake, of failing. It had been a natural reaction for a new and eager student. But this, this letter with its strange accusations had her pulse racing with a fear she didn't recognize.

She turned her attention to Clint. Head bent forward,

eyes narrowed, he seemed to be looking straight into the paper for clues as he read and reread.

"What do you think it means?" she asked him. "I mean, why would someone send this…"

"I don't know yet. But I'm sure as hell going to find out."

"It has to be a lie, Clint."

He didn't respond. Instead he snatched up the cream-colored envelope and held it to the light.

"That baby is Jane's," Tara assured him. "I know it as well as I know myself. Any woman can tell a mother and her child, especially a woman who…"

His attention severed for a moment, Clint turned to look at her. "A woman who what?"

Tara's heart stuttered, and she shifted from one foot to the other. Her mouth was unruly lately, no control—absolutely none. Clint didn't need to hear about the woman inside her who wished for a family, for a sweet child like Autumn.

"I'm just saying that I can spot the truth a mile away, always have," she amended. "And there's no doubt that Jane is Autumn's mother."

At first Tara thought that Clint was going to press her for a direct answer, but he didn't. He turned back to the letter. "I agree. I don't think this—" he held up the sheet of paper to the light once again "—has anything to do with the truth."

"Well, you're in this type of business, what do you think it's about? Is Jane in some kind of danger?"

"I think it's a backhanded threat," he said, finding her gaze once again.

Threats...

Fear moved through Tara, slow and heavy. It was strange. She could handle blood and chaos and needles. She could withstand days without sleep and nights of agonized cries at the bedsides of her patients. But when it came to the unknown, something she had no idea how to fix or control, she was lost.

And this situation made no sense. Why in the world would someone want to threaten Jane? Why such horrible accusations?

Clint's eyebrows furrowed with concern and he leaned toward her. "You're as white as a sheet, Tara."

She shook her head and lied. "I'm fine."

Turning her to face him, he put his hands on her shoulders. "You're not fine, you're shaking."

"It's *nothing*."

"It's natural to be frightened in a situation like this."

"I don't get frightened," she argued, trying to move away from him as her shakes turned to trembling.

But Clint held her firm. "You don't have to play that invulnerable, tough-skinned-nurse role with me. I'm not one of your patients."

"I'm not playing at anything—"

He never let her get further than that. With gentle force he pulled her into his arms.

Embarrassment filled her. Didn't he understand? *She* was the caregiver. *She* was the easer of feelings. Not the other way around—and not by Clint Andover.

But her will wasn't strong enough to resist his comfort. She didn't try to pull away. Instead she pressed closer, toward the heat of his body, the hard angles of his chest. He felt safe. So safe, and she didn't want to move, just breathe in the spicy scent of him. Pretend that they were alone together and that this was all a dream.

"Everything's going to be all right," he whispered against her hair.

Tara felt a lump form in her throat. It had been a long time since anyone had said that to her. And she really wanted to believe him. "Clint..."

"I swear it, Tara. No one's going to harm you."

"I'm not just worried for myself."

"I know."

For a moment she abandoned the safety of his chest and looked up at him. "What are we going to—"

"Shh..." He placed a finger to her lips. "You'll both be safe. You have my word."

His simple touch calmed her mind but aroused her senses. How did he have such an effect on her? she wondered, when his gaze dropped to her mouth. How could a woman want a man so much? she mused, as Clint brushed his thumb over her lips, back and forth.

Her mind leaped from the fear of a moment ago to wondering what that same sweet, insistent touch would feel like elsewhere, her cheek, her neck, the curve of her breast.

Tara sucked in a breath and forgot herself for a moment. She pressed her chest tighter against him.

Clint sucked in a breath. "Tara," he whispered, his tone husky, hungry.

"I need...I need..." She couldn't finish the sentence. She couldn't say it out loud or to herself.

Desire flashed in Clint's eyes as he gazed down at her, his free hand raking up her back, cupping the back of her neck. He was going to kiss her, she thought wildly. He was going to kiss her, make her breathless, make her lose her mind.

But he didn't lean in, didn't cover her mouth, just tightened his hold on the back of her neck.

He was fighting this, fighting her. Why, she didn't know.

"We need to be careful, Tara."

She looked at him. He at her. The double meaning in his words not at all lost on her. Easing out of his grasp, moving back a safe distance, she let the humiliation over her wanton behavior set in, let his words of warning sober her and bring her back to the present, and to the impact of the letter.

With a heavy sigh, Clint leaned against the kitchen counter, ran a hand through his hair. "I'm sorry, Tara. I suppose I should have told you that there was a possible danger here, but I thought it was better—"

"Told me?" she interrupted, instantly alert and awake now. "Told me what?"

"Several weeks ago someone tried to get into Jane's hospital room."

Tara's heart dropped into her shoes. "What?"

Clint shook his head. "I stopped him. But the bastard got away."

"Ohmigod."

Clint's eyes were hooded like a hawk's as he stared at her. "Someone tried to take Autumn from the hospital, as well."

"The baby?" she fairly choked, white-hot fear gripping her gut.

"Don't worry, she's safe with the Sorrensons."

"Tara?"

Tara's head was spinning as Jane called her from the balcony. She couldn't take it all in. The letter, Clint's wariness to kiss her and the new information he'd just slammed on her. Then there was the disintegration of her own restraint to deal with.

All of it threatened to overwhelm Tara, but she couldn't allow herself to fall apart. Not now. She would keep her cool, had to. Jane was still her patient and her responsibility.

"I'll be right up," Tara called, then turned to Clint and said firmly, "I'd better go to her."

He only nodded. "And I have work to do."

But he didn't make a move to go, didn't head for the door.

"You can go. We'll be fine," she assured him with a heavy heart. "I've got your cell phone number. I'll call you if anything comes up."

That same unease laced with heat glittered in his sapphire eyes. "I don't want to leave you."

Tara's pulse skittered, her breath, too. She knew

what he really meant, but the words, the intimate tone gripped her senses. "Jane and I will be all right."

He didn't look convinced. "The thing is, my assistant is out of town. I'm going to have to check this letter out myself."

"I understand. We need all the information we can get as soon as we can get it, right?"

"We?"

"You don't think I'm going to let you do this without me, do you?"

His gaze darkened, his tone along with it. "That's exactly what I think. Besides, I have plenty of help on this."

"Right." The glorious and infamous Texas Cattleman's Club. "But Jane and Autumn are my responsibility, too, Clint. Now that I'm aware there is some danger here, I'm willing to take the risk and help them."

"Tara, listen—"

She didn't want to hear it. "No. If you want my cooperation, you'll let me help you." She turned away from him, headed for the stairs.

But Clint grabbed her hand, and turned her back to face him. "I could have the two of you moved to my place in an hour if I wanted," he warned darkly, his lips tightening as he pulled her closer.

"But you won't," she countered, the heat between them from a moment ago rising to the surface once again, making Tara's knees a little weak. "You don't want to upset Jane. You don't want her to know about the letter and—''

He hesitated a moment before releasing her and backing away. "Fine. Fine. You win. For now.'' He stalked past her, went to the door. "Make sure this is locked up tight. I have two of my men out there guarding this place, but you can't be too careful.''

Her mouth dropped open. "Two men? When did you do that?''

"They've been here from the moment you brought Jane into this house.'' He raised a brow. "Night, Tara.''

"Good night,'' she muttered, feeling slightly nonplussed. It seemed he hadn't told her a few more important details. But regardless, she felt safer knowing that there were two highly trained sentinels watching over Jane.

"I'll see you in the morning,'' he called back before she shut the door.

"In the morning,'' she repeated softly as she leaned back against the cool wood and sighed. "And I hate myself for it, but I can't wait.''

He sat at his desk in the dark and stared out the window at the town he was beginning to despise. The people here were basic, without an ounce of sophistication. Luckily for him, they were also clueless.

Except for that group of wealthy cowboys that had foiled his first attempts at success.

Well, this time he wasn't sending his flunkeys to do

the job. This time the doctor was in charge. And if things went according to plan, he'd have what he came for and be on his way in just under two weeks.

A grin creased his mouth. No doubt the nurse had gotten his letter. She was a feisty creature, might cause a few problems, but he'd take care of that if the need arose.

Hell, he almost wished that it would....

To Clint Andover, the holidays were just like any other. Work, sport, more work. Christmas was no time to celebrate as he'd lost his taste for celebration three years ago, along with any semblance of faith he'd once possessed.

But Royal, Texas, didn't subscribe to his way of thinking, Clint couldn't help but notice as he drove through town the following night. As the sun set in the west, the festive twinkle lights came out, the scent of pine wafted in the crisp air and the cheerful faces of holiday shoppers filled the sidewalks and cafés.

There'd been a time when he was young, when his parents had been alive, that he'd lived for Christmas, the family dinners and the promise of Santa. He'd always hoped that someday he'd feel that again, that wonderment, that magic, through the eyes of his own children.

But as it was, he mused, pulling into Tara's driveway and giving his man a quick wave, ignoring the season altogether was the only way to get to January without losing his mind.

"Good evening, Mr. Andover." Looking exception-
ally pretty in a pale-pink sweater and killer-curve jeans,
Tara gave him a wide grin. "Three visits in one day.
You're something else."

"I do my best." His hands itched to reach for her,
take her in his arms and feel her against him. But he'd
had enough of that kind of trouble, enough distractions
over the past several days.

Holding the door open, she asked, "Would you like
to come inside? It's getting chilly out there."

"No thanks." He had plans, and they included her,
coming out, joining him.

"Okay... Any news on the letter?"

"Not yet."

"What's next, then?"

"Patience is a virtue, Nurse Roberts."

Her grin widened and she hooked a stray curl behind
her ear. "I wouldn't figure you for that particular virtue, Andover."

"No? What would you figure me for?"

"Hmm, tyrannical maybe?"

He leaned against the doorjamb, snorted. "I've said
it before and I'll say it again—trouble."

"That must be my virtue." Her musical laughter
echoed in the cold air, but warmed him to the core.
"So, if this isn't about the letter and you're not coming
in, can I assume—" she arched a brow "—this is a
social call?"

"As a matter of fact, it is. I thought I could take you
out to dinner."

"Payback for not telling me the whole truth about this situation?"

"Something like that." Something exactly like that, actually. It had been his thought on the way here, or his excuse for sharing a meal with her. He wasn't too interested in figuring out which.

"What about Jane?" Tara asked innocently.

"Marissa picked Jane up an hour ago."

Her pale lashes shot up with surprise. "How did you know that?"

He merely raised a brow. "One of my men followed her there. We don't fool around, Tara."

She blushed immediately. A pretty sight, but one that filled him with questions about where else she might blush. Not to mention a few lustful thoughts that ended with that pink sweater on the floor of his bedroom.

Through gritted teeth he asked, "You ready to go?"

"You know, this might look like a date."

"And?"

"Do we want the whole of Royal talking about us?"

"I couldn't give a damn, Tara. I've never cared what anyone thought." An accurate statement, and besides, as long as they both knew what tonight was really about, sharing a meal together, that's all that mattered to Clint.

A slow, impish smile spread over Tara's features, reminding him of that oh-so-sweet moment they'd shared last night. How her lips had felt against his fingers, soft, pouty—and in need of his mouth on hers if only he could let go of his resolve and give in to what they both wanted.

He and Tara had much in common it seemed. They were both afraid. She, of letting go of control. He, of needing anything or anyone.

But could they put that aside? Did they have to unravel and solve their respective issues to enjoy each other's company? Take what they were both so desperate to give?

He cursed silently. He didn't know. He just didn't know.

"So, what do you say?" he asked, offering her his hand.

She took it and smiled. "A burger at the diner sounds pretty good."

Five

"Evening, folks."

Sheila Foster, the Royal Diner's favorite waitress, not to mention the town's consummate busybody, grinned at Tara and Clint as they entered the packed restaurant.

"Table for two?" the blousy woman cooed, her usual overly tight, overly pink uniform now replaced with holiday red, the same shade as her lipstick.

"Yes, thanks." Tara tried to make her voice sound light, as if she was not the least bit unnerved by having the sweet and very funny woman eyeballing Clint and her as though they were really a couple.

But Clint was less interested in appearances. His

hand found the small of Tara's back as he asked Sheila, "Do you have anything by the window, pretty lady?"

The forty-something woman tossed Clint a wicked grin. "Anything for you, Clint, you know that."

"Anything but a date, right?"

Pretty lady? A date? Tara was too stunned to say a word. Was stoic Clint Andover actually flirting? And with a little added humor in there for good measure?

Whatever had unveiled this playful side of him, she liked it, wanted to see more of it and wished that she was the one who could bring it out of him—make him happy again...

"Sugar, as much as I'd love to teach you all I know about love, I just can't do it." She lowered her voice, spoke conspiratorially. "Have too many fishes dangling on the line as it is." Then with a quick wink, she motioned for them to follow her.

"I'd say more like one in particular," Clint chided, nodding in the direction of the kitchen.

Sheila snorted.

"Happy holidays, folks!" The diner's owner and cook, and Sheila's favorite fish, Manny Reno, stuck his head out of the kitchen and flashed them a smile.

Both Clint and Tara gave him a wave, then slipped into one of the booths lining the windows. It was a comfortable spot, near the jukebox. The old machine was dishing out forty-fives, at present, Nat King Cole's "A Christmas Song." One of Tara's favorites.

"So, what'll it be?" Sheila asked, pencil to pad. "Manny's serving up a terrific chili tonight."

Clint looked at Tara, his eyebrow raised in question. "I think we'll both have a burger and fries."

Tara nodded. "And mint chocolate shakes?"

The look that passed over Clint's face wasn't one of shock exactly. No, it was more along the lines of wonder and just a little curiosity. "How did you remember that?"

A laugh, quick and throaty bubbled up from her throat. "I don't know. It just popped into my head."

They hadn't shared a mint chocolate shake, but they'd sure talked about it being their favorite during that one wonderful night in the gazebo at Royalty Park. They'd kissed and cuddled and talked. They'd bantered on about kid stuff: favorite TV show, movie, food, sport, class in school—and of course, that favorite ice cream flavor.

"Would you like one shake, two straws?"

Startled, Tara glanced up. Popping her gum and smiling, Sheila wiggled her eyebrows.

"We'll take two shakes," Clint said dryly. "And two straws."

The woman winked. "Burgers, fries and two mint chocolate shakes coming up."

When Sheila had finally gone and was headed toward the kitchen, Clint eased back against the booth and chuckled. "That woman is a pistol."

"She sure is. You know she'll have our little shake conversation all over town by morning."

He shrugged. "I don't care about gossip and neither should you."

"I'm just trying to preserve your reputation, Andover," she explained, teasing him a little, hoping to keep that playful side of him alive.

"Really." He leaned toward her. "So...what are they saying about me around here?"

"Let's see," she glanced at the ceiling as though trying to recall. "I've heard that you're a sweet, sensitive man who looks both ways when he crosses the street and waves at all his neighbors."

"A real Boy Scout, huh?"

She nodded, adding sagely, "You see why I'm worried about sullying your reputation?"

His cobalt gaze swept over her. "Sounds to me like I need all the sullying I can get."

The din of customers chatting, music playing, pots and pans banging and the scent of meat cooking and potatoes frying—it all dissolved into a dull roar.

"I know someone who might be interested in the job," Tara said casually.

His gaze was bold as he tried to read her. "Who might that be?"

"Sheila, of course."

"Not my type."

She couldn't stop herself. "Who is your type?"

His gaze lowered, as did his voice. "I seem to have a thing for troublemakers."

Tara's pulse jumped in her blood, and she felt suddenly aware of what she was wearing underneath her sweater and jeans, as though Clint could see her white lace bra and panties, as though he could will them off her with just a glance.

She swallowed hard and forced herself to breathe. "Who would've thought that a mint chocolate shake could get us into such hot water twice?"

"Hot water?" he asked.

"Well, there's this stimulating round of…banter. And then there was that kiss in the gazebo."

His mouth tipped up at the corner, his voice remained low. "Right. But that was the kind of hot water a man likes to go swimming in."

Where was their food? she wondered madly, glancing toward the kitchen for some kind of interference, welcome or not. If that milkshake didn't get here soon, she couldn't be responsible for her actions.

Even the thought of leaning across the booth and demanding a kiss from this man didn't seem at all insane.

Oh, she was falling downhill hard and fast, that was certain.

But as she strained past Clint's handsome face for a better look at the restaurant, she didn't see her rescuer, Sheila, carrying out plates or glasses. No, what she saw had the warmth in her belly turning sour.

Dressed far more elegantly than a night out in Royal called for in a dark blue suit, neatly pressed, a crisp white shirt and a paisley tie was a tall, thin man standing at the counter, his expression one of contempt as he stared at the menu.

"More hot water…" she muttered to herself.

But Clint heard her and turned to look at what had caught her eye. His tone changed radically from low and husky to serious and alert. "Who is that?"

"That would be Dr. Belden."

"From the hospital?"

She nodded. "He's fairly new."

Clint turned around to face her. "Do I sense a hint of censure in your voice?"

"Yes."

"What's the problem?"

Tara gave a half shrug. "I've only dealt with him a few times. Each time he's been cool and arrogant. It's no secret that he has little respect for the nurses in the hospital, and I've heard he has little bedside manner with the patients. But it's not just that."

His blue eyes narrowed. "No?"

"There's something else, something I can't put my finger on."

At that moment Belden glanced her way. He seemed to recognize her at once and gave her an amiable nod.

Tara could do little but return the gesture as she ignored the shiver crawling up her spine.

"You were saying?" Clint prodded tensely.

Not sure what that something was that she couldn't put her finger on or what it meant—if anything—Tara was wholeheartedly thankful when Sheila sauntered toward them and set their burgers and milkshakes down on the table.

Determined to find that playful mood once again, Tara grabbed for the ketchup and forced a smile. "I'm sure it's nothing."

"Tara, hi, it's Jane. Autumn's acting kind of fussy tonight, so I've decided to stay over at David and Marissa's. You know how much I miss Autumn, and I really want to be here for her, hold her if she starts crying again. Say hello to Clint for me and I'll call you in the morning. Bye."

Tara pressed the erase button on her answering machine, then turned to Clint, who was standing next to the kitchen counter. "Jane says hi."

A flash of humor crossed his handsome face. "Yeah, I heard that."

Did he also hear how her heart had dropped into her shoes when she'd realized they'd come home to an empty house? she wondered. Could he have heard the way her pulse had leaped to life when she'd realized that the house would remain that way for the rest of the evening? No interruptions, no unwitting chaperone asleep in her room on the second floor.

No doubt misinterpreting her uneasy expression, Clint walked around the counter to her side and draped an arm over her shoulders. "Don't worry. She'll be safe with David. He's ex-military, too, doesn't mess around. And I have my man standing guard there, as well."

Her skin tingled at the contact. "I know."

"I'm not entirely sure about *you* though."

She looked up, confused. "What do you mean?"

"Here...alone..."

"Oh," she laughed, though it came out as more of a girlish giggle. "I'm fine."

He reached out and brushed a wisp of hair off her cheek. "Yes, you are."

The intimate touch made her knees soft as butter, but his tone lent an altogether different reaction. "Thank you, but—"

"But what?"

"You sounded almost angry giving me that compliment."

Pure frustration lit his eyes, and he turned around, ready to walk away. Then he released a heavy sigh, turned back to her and pulled her into his arms. "I am angry, dammit."

Tara could barely catch her breath he held her so close, but she managed to utter, "Why?"

"Don't you understand?" he growled. "I don't want this."

The closeness of him, his hip to her belly, the feel of his rock-hard chest molded against her, the brush of stubble on his stubborn jaw.

"This?" she stumbled. "Holding me, touching me? What?"

"You. I don't want to want you." His hands raked up her back, cupped her neck, made her look into his eyes.

Her pulse pounding, Tara stared up at him. She wanted to tell him that she was scared, too, that this thing between them blew her mind every time they were together.

She wanted to tell him that he'd opened up her romantic soul and let the tiger loose.

She wanted to tell him that she was close to giving up, giving in to its control, no longer willing to deny herself.

But he didn't offer her the opportunity.

He closed in, covering her mouth with a hot, hungry kiss that had electric shocks erupting in her belly. His hold on her tightened as his mouth switched angles.

Tara wanted to cry or cry out with the sweetness, the decadence of it all. But she refused to waste a single second.

As she returned his demanding kisses, her tongue teasing his, she fumbled for something to hold on to. She felt weak, out of her mind, and she grasped for the counter. But her hand skidded and she knocked a stack of papers and mail off the gray Formica.

The sound cut into their heated moment, and they both eased apart, looking and feeling guilty and totally on fire.

"I'm sorry," she mumbled stupidly. She had no words, no excuses for her behavior, her resistance to this thing that pulled them together.

Feeling awkward and clumsy and needing a moment out of the azure spotlight that was Clint's gaze, she bent to pick up the papers.

"Let me help you." Clint's voice was near to madness as he knelt beside her.

"That's not necessary, I—" She sucked in a breath as icy fear twisted around her heart. "Oh, God."

"What?"

Her hands shaking, Tara held up a long cream-colored envelope, one that looked exactly like the letter she'd received yesterday.

Curses fell from his mouth. "Let me open it."

She gave it to him. "Do you think I'm going to get one of these every day?"

Clint said nothing, just tore open the envelope.

"Will you read it out loud?" Tara asked, coming to her feet.

"No."

"Clint, I have a right to hear it. It's addressed to me."

"All right," he relented. He stood up beside her, then read from the letter. "'That bitch you're protecting is a liar and a thief…'"

"Oh, God," Tara breathed, her chest tightening.

Clint glanced up from the paper. "Whoever is sending these is pissed as hell."

"But at Jane and Autumn…why?"

"That's what I'm going to find out."

"Do you think this person could get…violent?"

Clint's lips thinned. "If pushed too far anything's possible."

Tara flinched. She was glad Jane was at David and Marissa's tonight. That she was safe, and that she knew nothing about what was happening.

"I need to get this to the lab," Clint said, regret

flashing in his eyes. "Check for prints. Hopefully, the perp got sloppy this time and left some sort of clue."

"Yes, of course." As selfish and as unlike her as it was, Tara didn't want him to go anywhere. Sure, there was a guard outside, but she wanted Clint, his warmth, his hands to comfort her.

The realization made her cringe.

For the first time in what seemed like forever, she wanted comfort. Not just a night or two of lovemaking until this mystery was solved.

She almost groaned aloud. She was no wimpy female, for heaven's sake. She needed to gain a little control over herself here.

Her chin lifted, Tara walked over to the door and held it open. "I hope you find something this time."

Clint didn't follow her. He sat down on the couch. "As I said, this needs to get to a lab. But I'm not taking it in."

"What?"

"I'm not taking the letter."

"But you have to, need to—and right now. We need the information as quickly as possible."

"And we will." He took out his cell phone, flipped the receiver into place, then pressed a button. "Doug, get over to 3351 Duncan Hill Road as soon as you can."

When he'd hung up and eased the phone back into his pocket, he looked up at her. "My assistant's back. He'll take the letter to the lab and process it tonight."

Tara didn't shut the door. The cold air seeped

through the tiny holes in the screen door like powdered sugar through a sieve. "If this is about protecting me—"

"So what if it is?"

With every ounce of self-control she had remaining, Tara gave him an imperious glare. "I told you I don't need it."

"And I told you to expect to have me around."

"That was for Jane—about Jane."

He held up the envelope that bore her name on the front, his eyes flashing blue fire. "This made it about you, too."

"I am fully capable—"

"It's done, Tara!"

She stopped, stared, her heart hammering in her chest.

"Let it go."

He was impossible. Yet so was she. Together they were like firecracker and flame. A heady combination in negotiations, compromise and matters of the heart.

She glowered at him, but shut the door. "I'm just going to head to bed anyway, I—"

"Go ahead."

"So...what?" she asked, walking toward him. "You'll just let yourself out when you're ready to leave?"

"I'm not going anywhere tonight. I'll take the couch."

Heat flooded her cheeks, not to mention the lower

half of her. He was staying here, overnight, feet from her bed. This had to be a test from above.

One she was very likely to fail.

"If you could spare a pillow and blanket…"

"Sure. Anything else?" she asked inanely.

"I think I'll be all right." He dropped his hands behind his head, leaned back against the couch and leveled her gaze with his. "Unless you're offering to tuck me in."

Six

She still slept in the same bed she'd had as a teenager. The pine four-poster she'd seen in a magazine when she was twelve and had saved every penny of her allowance to buy.

Her mother had thought it a wise and practical purchase, but to Tara it had been all about indulgence. A place she could escape to at night, where she could dream and wish and be anything she wanted.

The one spot where she could set aside her sense of duty for a while.

But tonight, lying under the pale-blue sheets, she felt anything but comfortable.

And she certainly couldn't escape.

A man was in her house.

Clint Andover ruled her brain as well as her bed, and he'd barely touched her. Perhaps it was the promise of that touch. Perhaps it was the scent of him, clean and masculine tickling her senses long after she'd left him with pillow and blanket on the couch.

Perhaps it was the image of him, hands behind his head, bare-chested.

Tara's skin went hot, then cold, as a desperate hunger she'd come to know so well moved through her blood. Frustrated, she leaned over and glanced at the bedside clock.

One-thirty.

She groaned. Hours to go before dawn. How was she supposed to get any sleep with these thoughts and sensations ruling her?

What about Clint, she wondered. Was he asleep? Or was he stretched out on his back, one muscled arm behind his head having the same problem?

Tara shook her head and glanced heavenward. Was she really going to find out?

The devil took hold of the angel she wanted so much to remain and forced her up and out of bed.

The house was scented with her.

Vanilla and something floral, designed to make a man go mad with need if inhaled too long.

Clint shifted on the couch, which incidentally was too short for a man of his size. Not that it really mattered, considering he had no intention of sleeping. First because he was waiting for his assistant to call back with any results on the letter, and second because he wasn't about to wake up in Tara Robert's home in a cold sweat from his ongoing nightmare.

Soft footfalls curbed his internal dialogue, and he listened as they made their way down the hall and toward the kitchen.

A very feminine-sounding sneeze echoed through the still house.

Clint grinned broadly but didn't move from his spot on the couch. "Late-night craving?"

There was a quick gasp, then "Excuse me?"

Reaching behind him, Clint turned the lamp one click. A pale, soft light filled the room. "I wouldn't have figured you for the late-night-snack type."

She didn't respond immediately, and Clint wondered if she had run in silent retreat back to her room. But then her face appeared over the top of the couch.

"Normally I'm not," she said.

She looked so pretty with no makeup, her green eyes shone bright and warm, her honeyed hair falling loose about her shoulders in relaxed curls.

But all that innocence and simplicity fell away as his gaze traveled lower.

The simple white cotton nightgown she wore was just a little bit transparent, showing off the drop-dead silhouette beneath. Clint's hands itched to reach out and grab her, lift her over the back of the couch and into his arms.

"Do you have a craving tonight, Tara?" he asked

without thinking, then wished to God he could steal the sensual query back. But it was too late.

The soft light from the lamp illuminated the touch of eagerness that passed over her eyes. But she didn't rise to his bold query.

"I thought I'd make some hot chocolate," she said, glancing back toward the kitchen.

He nodded. "Sounds good."

"Can I make you a cup, too?"

He wasn't in the mood for hot chocolate. "Sure. Can I help?"

"No, I've got it all under control," she said, walking into the kitchen.

"Words to live by, huh?"

She stuck her head around the corner. "For me or for you, Andover?"

"For us both I think."

"Yes." She disappeared back into the kitchen. "Gets awfully tiring sometimes."

"What's that?" Clint got up and followed her. "Staying in control?"

"I'm afraid control was a necessary evil as a child. My lifestyle demanded it."

She stood in front of the stove, the kitchen light above her, providing a new and more exciting view of what was under that white cotton nightgown.

"And now?" he asked, his body hardening under his T-shirt and jeans as he took in the slip of panties and the curve of her breast. "Does your lifestyle still demand that you remain in control?"

His certainly did.

Tara's hand shook as she filled the kettle with water. "To be honest, I'd love to take a few days off."

Leaning against the kitchen counter, Clint asked the question he'd asked of himself too many times to count. "And what would you do in those few days?"

"Breathe, be selfish. Allow myself to take without any accountability." She was quiet as she emptied the contents of two hot chocolate packets into fat mugs. "I don't know why I'm saying this."

"I hear that after midnight you can be vulnerable without censure." He frowned, as that piece of advice was a little too close to home.

"I wish that were true," she said.

"It can be."

"Just between us though, right?"

Her eyes were playful, but her words had his chest in a vise. He resented this hold she had over him. Yet, when it came to actually resisting her, face-to-face, he was utterly powerless.

She moved toward him, her gaze on the drawer his hip was blocking. "Excuse me. Need to get a spoon."

But he didn't move. He took her hand and eased her to him. With his legs splayed wide, she moved into place against his groin, fitting perfectly.

Clint wanted to growl at the feeling of her pliable softness against the growing steel in his jeans. He was no saint when it came to women. He liked being with them, enjoyed their softness, their scent. Of course, he treated them with respect, made sure they understood in advance that he could only be theirs for the night.

But with this woman things weren't that simple....

Instinct warned him that one night wouldn't be enough. It was why he'd tried to remain impassive around her. A goal that had failed miserably.

Clint lifted Tara's palm to his lips, kissed the sweet flesh there and uttered against her skin, "You can be anything with me, say anything."

"Is that the rule, Andover?" she asked, her voice husky.

"The promise," he corrected.

What was he saying? He didn't make promises.

"Well, in that case," Tara said, the warmth of her breath on his neck giving him electric chills. "Is there anything you'd like to say, anything you'd like to get off your chest?"

The hideous scar on that chest, his chest, twitched, the pain a deep one—one he wasn't willing to expose, even with her. One that was supposed to remind him to steer clear of intimate, highly sensual, needful situations like this.

But that scar's power was seized.

"We can't stop this from happening, can we?" she asked, looking up at him, her eyes as bright as two emeralds.

"I don't think so."

"Then maybe we should just let it run its course."

"Maybe." For the first time in his life, Clint wasn't sure what to do, where to begin. He wanted to give her all that she desired, that freedom to take, that chance to breathe and breathe deeply.

Hell, he wanted it, too.

But when she reached up and splayed her hands on his chest, he forgot for a moment and went a little mad. He didn't allow women to touch him there, not on his skin, not through a shirt. It was his shame, his scar of a past he would never let himself forget. And he reacted without thinking.

With gentle force he took her wrists in his hands and circled her arms behind her back.

But she didn't pull away as he thought she might. She moved closer, her mouth a breath away from his, her breasts jutting out as her back arched.

"I know about your scar," she whispered.

He shuddered with need, shuddered with pain. That night, the fire—it was common knowledge to all of Royal. But his scar— "How could you know?"

Her voice took on a gentle tone. "I worked in the burn unit a few months after…the accident."

"And the nurses all talk to each other, is that it?" he asked tightly.

"No. No." Her gaze flickered to his lips, then returned to his eyes. "It was only in relation to another case."

On a dry chuckle, he muttered, "Another disfigured member of society, huh?"

She looked startled, and she stiffened against him. But only for a moment. Then from beneath long lashes her green eyes flashed and her mouth curved into a smile. "If I remember correctly," she said, her sweet breath moving over his face, "the only thing the nurses could talk about was your fine physique and how they had insisted you have two full-body sponge baths every day to observe it."

Clint tightened his grasp on her. How did she do it? How did she disarm him, make his anger dissipate in seconds, leaving only admiration and desire in its wake?

Without answering his silent query, he leaned in, took her bottom lip between his teeth and suckled hard.

A moan escaped her throat, but she managed to utter, "I won't touch it, Clint. I won't touch you there. Not until you ask me to."

"I'll never ask you, Tara."

He captured her mouth in a hungry kiss, desperate to shut her up but crazy to taste her. Any minute now she was going to realize that they were making a huge mistake here and pull away from him. But until then he was going to enjoy that vanilla, floral scent of her as he covered her mouth, teasing her lips, welcoming her tongue.

There were no games to her kiss, no pride in her movement, he thought as she pressed her hips against his shaft, wiggled and squirmed. She was hungry, and hungry for him, and it felt damn good to be wanted like this.

"Clint…"

"Don't think, Tara," he uttered hoarsely. "For both our sakes, don't think."

He dropped her wrists, raked his hands up her back and neck, then plunged them into her hair. They kissed long and wet, lingering over each other. She tasted so sweet, so forbidden, and he knew he'd never get enough of her.

He was lost in the madness of the moment. He didn't care what happened tomorrow or the next day or five minutes from now. He allowed instinct to drive him. And if it led him to ruin, so be it.

With a wolfish groan he skimmed his hands down her torso to her waist and pulled the hem of her night-gown up her legs. Every inch of taut, smooth skin he encountered made him harder, made his chest constrict with a want he hadn't felt in a long time. Up, up, he skimmed her thighs until he cupped her through her thin cotton panties.

Tara stilled for a moment, sucking in a breath, then she thrust her hips forward, pressing herself into his hand.

Clint nearly died right there. As even through the fabric, he felt how ready she was, for him, his hand, his mouth…

Beside them, the water boiled rapidly on the stove.

If she made one move, one gesture toward her bed-room or the couch or the rug beside the dark fireplace, he wouldn't be able to quell his need.

But she didn't move. She didn't have the chance.

The irritating jingle of his cell phone made the decision for them.

Clint cursed darkly.

"You need to get that, don't you?" she asked, her voice low and raspy with unfulfilled desire.

Again he cursed and moved away from her. "It's my assistant. I told him to call as soon as the lab results were back from the letter."

"You need those results."

His nostrils flared. "What I need is—"

"No," she interrupted. "Don't say it."

The shrill ring of his cell phone echoed through the house.

"Answer the phone, Clint."

Duty wrestled with desire inside him, but he gave in to the one he knew so well—the one that ruled him.

Pushing away from the counter, he stalked over to the couch, to the maddening ring, his jaw as tight as the rest of him and barked out a terse "Hello" into his cell phone.

And got the answer he didn't want.

"Sorry, boss. The letter was clean."

The following day Tara picked up Jane at the Sorrensons' and they headed into town for a little Christmas shopping. The weather was cool, no wind and lots of sunshine. The perfect day to park the car and stroll Royal's Main Street looking for bargains, that unique present or new ornament for the tree.

For Tara, she'd suggested this outing in the hopes it would take her mind off last night.

If that was possible.

Clint's mouth, his kiss, his touch, her reaction...how

she'd wanted more. But what she gave herself was all she thought she deserved—the cold, lonely crispness of her blue cotton sheets.

After hearing the results of the phone conversation with his assistant, Tara had left the kitchen and Clint and headed to bed. The four-poster had never felt so big or so empty before. But it had been her only shelter from the constant nagging in her head about what was right and what was wrong and from the hunger that still resided in her at this very moment.

Clint hadn't knocked on her door. Perhaps he regretted their encounter or was, like her, unsure of what, if anything, to do about it.

But he'd been gone by the time she'd woken up from her fitful, dream-filled sleep. And that was probably a good thing, as she had no more answers today than she did last night. Only one conclusion: she'd never felt so wonderful as she'd felt in his arms.

Clint had left a note, however, letting her know that he was going to check out some leads today, and that there was still a guard watching her house.

She'd read the note three times, wanting to kick herself for hoping that a PS would suddenly appear at the bottom, saying that he'd see her tonight or some such nonsense. But it didn't.

"What a beautiful day."

Jane's cheery declaration tugged Tara back to the present. "It is pretty. I like it cold. Makes it more festive, you know?"

Jane nodded, then stopped in front of the drugstore

and pointed excitedly at the old-fashioned train set in the window. "That's sweet."

"How many people do you need to shop for?"

"I've got a small amount of money from the diaper bag I had at the Royal Diner and I'd like to get David and Marissa a gift. Maybe something for Harry."

"Harry?" Tara said, her brows knitting together.

Smiling, Jane turned and pointed to the man who was casually following them. "My bodyguard."

"Right. How could I forget Harry?" Tara grinned. "All righty. So we got David, Marissa and Harry. Anyone else?"

"And of course, my Autumn."

"Of course."

"She must have a few things."

"More than a few," Tara declared as they continued walking.

Jane laughed, her breath making puffy, filmy shapes in the cold. "How about you?"

"Just a couple of small things for the nurses at Royal Hospital, I think."

"Is that it?"

"Well, I have to pick up something for you and Autumn, too."

Jane looped her arm through Tara's as they wove in an out of the crowds. "Your friendship is more than enough for me."

"Well, that's too bad," Tara stated on a merry chuckle. "You're getting something whether you like it or not."

"Okay, okay."

Smiling and pointing at all the beautiful and festive town decorations, they headed across the street toward a small clothing boutique.

"So," Jane continued, "the nurses and me and Autumn...anyone else on your Christmas list? A handsome someone, perhaps?"

Pausing outside the shop, Tara studied her new friend. "You're actually smirking, Jane."

"Someone who's been more nice than naughty?"

"What?" Tara fairly choked.

"Or maybe the other way around," Jane said with a wink.

Tara's mouth dropped open. "Am I blushing or is it the cold?"

They both burst out laughing. Goodness, it felt wonderful to have a girlfriend, Tara mused. Someone to have this kind of fun, frolic. It had been years since she'd welcomed a true friend into her life, and she was glad it was Jane.

"So," Jane said, giving her a little nudge in the ribs. "What do you think Clint would like for Christmas?"

"I have no idea."

"I could think of a few things."

Well, to be honest, so could Tara. That is, if she allowed herself to. Sure, she'd kept all erotic images from erupting in her head today, but try as she might she couldn't get the sensations of last night's encounter to die down. Confusion, tingling skin, heat and the pull in her belly. Lips plump and just a little raw from his kiss and from years of neglect.

Lord, the realities of losing control weren't easy to handle.

"So?"

Tara glanced up right into Jane's probing violet eyes. "What?"

"Present? For Clint?"

She laughed. "You're too much, Jane."

Jane just grinned wider. "I see you, big red bow and nothing else."

Tara gasped in mock surprise. "You've got a little of the bad girl in you, Jane."

"I think you may be right." She tossed Tara a tight smile. "I wish I could remember."

"You will. I promise." With a nod for extra emphasis, Tara tugged Jane toward the store. "Let's head into the boutique, and I'll think about the bow."

"All right."

"Remember, we need to get a tree, too."

"Oh, a tree," Jane cried out gaily, her spirits once again soaring. "With ornaments and candy canes and cookie bells and stars?"

"And an angel on top."

The playful look in Jane's eyes morphed into one of affection and familiarity. "Thanks for helping me, Tara. Your friendship, your reassurance, and all this homey stuff, it means the world to me."

Tara's heart squeezed. "Your friendship means the world to me, too."

After a quick hug, they headed up the steps to the boutique. But Tara held back for a moment. She'd felt something, someone watching her. It was an uncomfortable, unnatural feeling that made her palms sweat against the banister.

Letting Jane go ahead of her, she paused at the shop door and glanced around. At first she saw nothing out of the ordinary. Just shoppers and business folks, and she couldn't help but wonder if her feelings were due to the impact of the letters or the presence of Harry the bodyguard.

But then she spotted him. Standing outside the bookstore, his dark eyes fixed on her.

Dr. Beldon.

The look between them lasted only a moment, as he didn't stay in front of the bookstore. He turned away and headed down the street. But the impact of that look gripped and held Tara hostage.

Why, she couldn't understand.

"Tara, you coming?" Jane called from inside the boutique.

Her friend's voice cut the tether that bound her to Beldon, and she could breathe again. Forcing a lightness she didn't feel into her voice, she called back, "Right behind you."

And ignoring the shiver traveling up her spine, she took a deep breath and followed Jane into the store.

Seven

———

The two letters stared up at Clint, mocking him in the predawn light that filtered through the windows of the TCC clubhouse. He'd called an emergency meeting only thirty minutes ago, but unlike most, these men hadn't uttered one complaint about the hour. Instead they'd rushed over, Stetsons dropped atop mussed hair, eyes slightly dazed, but ready for action.

"So, no fingerprints? No hair fibers?" Ryan asked, his dark brows lifting expectantly as he leaned against the pool table. "Nothing to link us to the bastard sending these threats?"

Clint scrubbed a hand over his stubbled jaw. "Not a damn thing."

"This fool is going to be real sorry he took us on," Alex muttered darkly.

With a derisive snort of agreement, David fell into a leather armchair.

Clint took a swallow of ink-black coffee, attempting to burn the curses bubbling in his throat. How in the hell could he have no leads, with two letters and two on-site kidnapping attempts at the hospital? He'd been involved in this type of work for years, and had never been this stumped.

And it was plain that he wasn't the only one who was feeling the pressure. Not to mention the frustration. These were men who were used to being in control, having control under all circumstances, and they were ready to go to just about any lengths for some answers.

"I have my best men working on this," Clint assured them. "I'll get to the bottom of it."

David nodded, leaning back in the leather armchair. "We know."

"Hell, even if it means living at Tara's until this whole business is resolved," Clint muttered to himself.

But the men heard him. Alex tossed him a grin. "That's commitment to the cause, man."

Ryan chuckled. "Real dedication."

Clint shot each of his friends a black gaze before turning toward the windows. He didn't want them to see the vein that throbbed in his temple and neck. Just the thought of the emerald-eyed nurse, sharing space with her, sharing a bed with her, had his pulse pounding.

Lines were blurring here, he thought, raking a hand through his hair. Raw desire and the desire to protect were fusing together.

He drained his coffee cup, barely tasting the extra-strength blend. Whatever was happening between him and Tara, he had to keep his eye on the ball. He couldn't allow another woman in his life to get hurt, not one he'd sworn to protect. So even if he stayed at her house, he had to try like hell to keep it business.

He glanced at the clock. Tara was pulling an all-nighter at the hospital. Maybe he'd head over there now, relieve his men for a few hours, stay with Jane and wait for Tara to come home.

"If no one has anything more," Clint said, turning back to face the men of the TCC, "let's pick this up later."

"I think we're done here," David said, rising from his chair.

Ryan nodded, while Alex said, his face a mask of aplomb, "Say hello to your nurse for us?"

"No," Ryan corrected vehemently. "'Mornin' ma'am' is far better at this hour."

Through gritted teeth Clint said, "You're two of the biggest horse's asses in Royal, you know that?" Then he pitched his coffee mug onto the table and stalked out the door.

"Annie, did you switch Mr. Young's IV?"

The plump brunette nurse gave Tara a quick smile. "Sure did."

"Great, thanks."

The hospital was fairly quiet that morning. The seven patients on the floor were either eating breakfast or resting. So it was the perfect time to write the morning report, which Tara was doing in rapid fashion.

Something that didn't go unnoticed by an eager-eyed Annie.

"You're in a hurry," she said, leaning against one of the pale blue sides of the nurses' station, a diet soda in her hand.

"Just want to get home and check in on Jane."

"How's she doing?"

"Good. Better." For a moment Tara wondered if her guest's spirits would remain as high if she found out about the letters they'd received. Odds were she wouldn't.

"So," Annie began, her blue eyes twinkling, her voice low in case the young, male unit clerk on the other side of the desk was trying to get an earful. "Is Mr. Gorgeous still looking out for her?"

"Who?" Tara asked lightly, keeping her gaze on the report.

"Clint Andover."

"Who?" Tara couldn't help but grin.

Annie chuckled. "Yeah, right."

"He looks out for her, yes." He looks out for both of us, Tara wanted to say, but thought it best to keep that information to herself.

"At your place?" Annie pursued.

Tara nodded.

"Well, isn't that cozy."

Donald, the unit clerk, glanced up then. Annie gave him a frown. "Doesn't involve you, Donald."

The young man blushed and immediately resumed his work.

Keeping her voice to a whisper, Tara amended, "It's actually more of a problem."

Annie almost choked on her swallow of soda. "Gorgeous man in the house. Protecting, surveying, sleeping in nothing but his boxers. Hon, I'd like that kind of problem."

Though she had a mild case of embarrassment, laughter bubbled in Tara's throat. Annie may be a nosy nurse, but her wicked ways were all in good fun and good friendship. She didn't have a malicious bone in her body, and Tara cared for her a great deal.

In fact, the nurses at Royal were the closest thing Tara had to family, maybe ever would. And the loyalty they displayed toward each other, not to mention the care they showed to their patients, truly set them apart from other staff and from other people.

Tara felt proud to be around them.

"Looks like Mr. Gorgeous might have some competition," Annie whispered, then proceeded to finish off her soda and toss it in the recycling.

"Competition?" Tara asked, confused.

"Yep." Annie nodded behind her. "From Dr. Mystery over there."

Tara glanced over her shoulder, expecting more of Annie's jokes, expecting to see one of the docs that had been around forever. Maybe Dr. Berg, who was going on seventy-five and had a permanent case of bad breath. But Annie's observation wasn't a practical joke or a quip.

Standing rigidly beside the elevator was none other than Dr. Beldon. And he was looking straight at Tara. Casually observing her, his gaze dark and severe.

"That man gives me the willies," Annie whispered.

"Yesterday and now today," Tara murmured more to herself than to anyone.

Annie leaned in close, as Donald was again interested in their conversation. "What happened yesterday?"

"I saw him in town. Actually I've seen him around town a few times lately."

Annie shrugged. "Well, Royal isn't all that big. Heck, you're bound to run into yourself from time to time."

"Yeah, that's true…"

Tara wasn't at all sure of her fellow nurse's assessment of the situation. But she was sure of one thing: Beldon was interested in her, for whatever reason. And it made her very uncomfortable.

As the man stepped into the elevator, and the door slid closed behind him, Annie muttered, "Maybe he has the hots for you, Tara."

"Lord, I hope not."

"He's not all that bad looking."

"No, he's not. But he's certainly no—" Tara wanted to bite her tongue. Hard. So she could never speak again. She prayed that Annie would just let her incomplete statement slide.

But that was too much to hope for.

The nurse grinned widely. "He's no Clint Andover, is that what you were about to say, hon?"

Tara took a deep breath, shook her head. "I have work to do."

"You always have work to do, Tara. Make some time for pleasure, okay?"

The woman's words seemed to echo the music in Tara's heart as of late—ever since a tall, dark and dangerously handsome security firm CEO came along and rattled her steady cage.

But what would mindless pleasure bring her?

Instant gratification, yes. A lifetime of wondering finally revealed, yes. Clint's mouth and hands and skin on her for one night, maybe two—yes.

Was all that worth the almost certain heartbreak to come if she gave in to such temptation? Because that's exactly what would happen. Clint was a broken man who fought getting close, letting go, even more than she did. Shoot, he wouldn't even allow her to touch his scar.

There was no future there.

Only present.

But could she grab hold of that, knowing that as soon as the mystery with Jane was solved, their romance would be over?

The sudden buzz of the call button tore Tara from her thoughts, and from an answer.

Annie smiled, gripped Tara's shoulder. "I'll get it. You head home."

"You sure?"

"No problem, hon."

Tara smiled at her friend. "Hey, I'm guessing that's Mr. Carey in 102. He's hit the call button ten times since five."

"He's the butt grabber, right?"

Tara laughed. "Right."

"Well, thanks for the warning," Annie said dryly. "And thanks for the advice. I mean it."

Annie nodded, then pushed away from the nurses' station and headed off toward 102.

Tara watched her go. If she only knew, Tara thought, her belly warming. If Annie only knew about the other night in the kitchen with Clint, how for a moment she'd given in to that pleasure, reveled in the man's scent and taste and touch.

It was close to 10:00 a.m. when Tara pulled into the driveway of her house. As she'd been inside the hospital all night, she hadn't been able to notice how the weather had turned. The sky was streaked with gray, and a deep chill hung in the air, ready to grow colder as the day wore on.

A nice change for Christmas, Tara mused as she climbed out of her car and trudged up the steps. Bone-weary, all she wanted to do was check on Jane then take a really hot shower.

When she walked through the front door, she fully

expected to find her friend making breakfast or having a shower of her own. But that was not the case. It wasn't Jane cooking omelettes and frying bacon.

"Morning, Nurse Roberts."

Clint stood in the kitchen in T-shirt, jeans and bare feet. He looked sexy as sin, and even tired as she was, Tara thought how wonderful it would be if she could just throw caution to the wind, run up to him and wrap her arms around his neck.

"I didn't see your car outside," she said, taking off her coat and hanging it in the hall closest. "How did you get—"

"My assistant dropped me off. His car's in the shop."

"Oh."

"Didn't mean to surprise you like that."

"You didn't. I mean, it's fine." Tossing her purse on the hall table, she walked through the living room and into the kitchen. "Cooking?"

He shrugged. "Thought you could use some breakfast."

"That was nice, very considerate. But you didn't have to—"

"I wanted to, Tara." He stood before her, imposing, serious and so amazingly good-looking. "No big deal, just breakfast."

But it was a big deal. To Tara at any rate. In all her adult years, she'd never had a meal made for her, except in a restaurant. And never by a man who looked at her as this one did, as though he'd like to have her for breakfast if she wouldn't mind.

That thought sent a wave of heat to her belly and a tingling sensation to her breasts.

Pushing away the longing in her blood, Tara watched as Clint divided the omelette dripping with melted cheese, then place each piece on a plate. Perfectly cooked bacon followed.

"Orange juice?" he asked.

"Sure."

This was a strange feeling, she mused. This whole breakfast-making scenario. She loved it, yet accepting it made her feel somehow…vulnerable. As though if she took what he was offering, she'd lose complete control over herself. Maybe tell him how he made her feel and beg him to make her feel that way again, come what may.

Clint Andover had stripped her of all sense and left a wanton, mindless, needful creature in its place.

"Why don't you take a seat at the table?" He handed her two glasses of orange juice. "Probably be more comfortable than eating at the kitchen counter."

"Should I wake Jane up, see if she'd like to share this feast?" Jane would be good right now. A sort of buffer, a reminder of why this handsome chef with his bare feet was really in her home.

"Jane's not here."

"What?" The OJ glasses wobbled when she set them down on the table.

"It's all right, Tara. She was up early and wanted to

see Autumn, so my assistant and I took her over to the TX S Ranch. I thought I'd stay, but Sorrenson's home today. He said he was going to watch her like a hawk. And we thought it might be wise if I was here, with you. In case another letter came.''

Her heart faltered. ''Oh, of course.''

''So, it's just you and me,'' he said, setting two plates laden with food on the table, ''sharing this feast.''

''Right.'' Just you and me alone. Again. Under the guise of protection and investigation, of course. ''Can I get anything else? Do we need forks?''

''No.'' He held up the utensils. ''Please sit down, you look exhausted.''

''I am.'' For many reasons, she mused silently.

Tara dropped into the chair, then dove into her breakfast. ''I had no idea you could cook.''

''Is bacon and eggs really cooking?''

''It is for a guy.''

He paused, fork halfway to mouth and raised an indignant brow in her direction.

''What…?'' she asked innocently.

''That was incredibly sexist.''

Tara paused for a moment, ran the conversation back through her head, then shook her head and chuckled. ''You're right. I'm sorry.''

He waved his fork at her. ''No big deal.''

''I guess I just don't see you as someone who likes the kitchen.''

''I don't. But with the right motivation.'' His gaze

didn't waver from hers. "A man will do just about anything."

Alarm bells rang in her head, and her heart. But it sure didn't stop her from asking, "The right motivation?"

"A hungry, tired and very beautiful woman who's been caring for others all night long, maybe for a lifetime." He reached over to her plate, broke a piece of bacon in half and held it to her lips. "Maybe she deserves a little care herself."

Like an obedient child, Tara opened her mouth and took the bite of smoky bacon.

Clint's gaze went dark blue, and so hypnotizing she nearly tossed aside the table settings and food and reached for him. This was like some kind of ridiculous fantasy anyway. Clint Andover, her childhood crush, sitting before her in jeans and a black T-shirt that showed off his muscular arms to perfection, feeding her breakfast, talking to her as though she were his woman.

Would it really be any more insane if she reached for him, pulled him to her and kissed him blind?

"Something on your mind, Tara?" he asked, returning to his breakfast.

Something? Try many things. "Nope."

"Then dig in. You need to eat."

With a dry mouth that wanted only the moisture of the man across from her, Tara did as he commanded. The omelette was delicious, light and fluffy and filled with cheese. And then there was the bacon. Crispy and very tasty, although nothing compared to the bit that Clint had fed her.

But she tried not to think too much, ate until she was full, then leaned back and smiled.

"Thank you. It was wonderful." She touched her belly. "I'm so full."

"And tired I'm willing to bet?"

"Yeah."

"Then how about a bath before bed?"

A soft gasp escaped her. "Excuse me?"

"A bath? Don't women love them?" He stood up, but kept her gaze. "All those bubbles and soaking for hours?"

She stared at him as her pulse pounded in her throat. "Yes, I guess some women do."

"But not you?"

Last time she'd taken a bath was when she was a kid. She'd never had the time, never made the time for such a thing. "It just always seemed like sort of a time waster."

"Didn't you say the other night that you'd like some time off to breathe, be free of all that?"

"I don't remem—"

"Sure, you do." His eyes were intent, daring her. "I'm going to get you in a bathtub, Tara."

Tara's mouth literally dropped open.

With just a slash of a smile, Clint abandoned the table and headed for the first-floor bathroom. "Maybe one of us can let go of their control," he called out to her.

"Yeah? And why does it have to be me?" she returned boldly, starting as she heard the bath water running.

He was serious, she thought, sitting up a little straighter in her chair—as if that would protect her from Clint Andover's ministrations. Running a bath for her?

She fought back the hysterical giggle that threatened to erupt from her throat. But she couldn't fight the quiver at the apex of her thighs or the rush of warmth that accompanied it.

"You're ready, capable of letting go, Tara."

She jumped. "What?"

"Come in here," he commanded over the rushing water.

Her heart jolted. "What about the dishes?"

"I'll take care of them."

On legs filled with water, she stood up and walked to the bathroom. She stood in the doorway and tried not to appear unnerved.

But it was no easy feat.

The lights were off, two candles she'd had in the storage closet for emergencies were lit. The scent of vanilla shower gel wafted through the air. Clint stood by the bathtub, which was laden with bubbles.

Tara nearly turned and ran.

The truth was, romance had never entered this house. Bubble baths were unnecessary. Candles and soap were practical items. And sexy beasts didn't cook breakfast and draw baths for weary nurses.

Until today.

Candlelight flickered in his dark eyes. "Don't try to analyze this, Tara."

"I'm not—"

"You are. Just accept it."

She inhaled deeply. "Are you…" She couldn't ask. Yet she could not ask. "Are you staying?"

"No."

She stiffened her spine. "Oh."

"This is for you. All that I can offer at the moment." He said the words with no apology, only blatant reality. "Now, take off those scrubs and get in the water."

She moistened her lips but didn't say anything, didn't move. It was hard to tell where her pounding pulse was coming from, as she heard it hammering everywhere.

Clint walked to her, stood in front of her, said bluntly, "I can help you, if you'd like."

Tara sucked in a breath as a deep throb pulsed between her legs. He would undress her, help her into the bath, then leave. It was a horrid deal, but she didn't want him to go just yet. Heaven help her, she wanted him to ease her clothes from her body, one at a time. She wanted to see his face, his eyes as he went. She wanted to see if he was affected at all.

"I'd like your help," she uttered hoarsely as though she'd just made a deal with the devil.

A spark of desire flamed in his eyes. "Put your arms over your head."

Tara hesitated just for a moment, uncertainty moving

through her, as she'd never exposed herself like this before. But with her muscles tight, clenched, she did as he instructed. She lifted her arms over her head.

She heard his breath roughen as his hands grazed her waist, as slowly he lifted the blue scrub top over her head, leaving only the thin white shell beneath it.

He lifted an eyebrow, his voice pained and husky. "Should I continue?"

Madness rose up to claim her—or was it just the real Tara surging to the surface for the first time? She didn't know, didn't care. She wanted her skin to breathe and be seen by this man.

Again she lifted her arms. Again, he rid her of a piece of clothing. The shell dropped to the floor.

"I'm not going to stop until you tell me to," he said, his hands at her back, fingers poised over the clasp of her bra.

Her breathing labored, she nodded.

With a click he released the clasp, then reached around and cupped her shoulders. Gently he inched off the straps. Her only thought was how amazing his hands felt on her skin as the white lace fell to the floor by her feet.

She felt warm air hit her breasts, and she closed her eyes and sighed.

"Finish it," she said, knowing that his gaze was on her, knowing that it was him and not the air that made her nipples stand up so hard and proud.

She heard him release a growl, low and hungry. She

NO POSTAGE
NECESSARY
IF MAILED
IN THE
UNITED STATES

BUSINESS REPLY MAIL
FIRST-CLASS MAIL   PERMIT NO. 717-003   BUFFALO, NY

POSTAGE WILL BE PAID BY ADDRESSEE

SILHOUETTE READER SERVICE
3010 WALDEN AVE
PO BOX 1867
BUFFALO NY 14240-9952

Get FREE BOOKS and a FREE GIFT when you play the...

LAS VEGAS
GAME

Just scratch off the gold box with a coin. Then check below to see the gifts you get!

YES! I have scratched off the gold Box. Please send me my **2 FREE BOOKS** and **gift for which I qualify**. I understand that I am under no obligation to purchase any books as explained on the back of this card.

326 SDL DUYF   225 SDL DUYV

FIRST NAME

LAST NAME

ADDRESS

APT.#

CITY

STATE/PROV.

ZIP/POSTAL CODE

(S-D-03/03)

7	7	7	Worth TWO FREE BOOKS plus a BONUS Mystery Gift!
			Worth TWO FREE BOOKS!
			TRY AGAIN!

Visit us online at
www.eHarlequin.com

felt his fingers on her waist, felt him ease down her scrubs until only her white cotton panties remained.

"Tara..." he uttered hoarsely.

She opened her eyes then, found him a foot away, his gaze menacing, like a starving animal who refused to take nourishment.

"Bath's getting cold," he muttered harshly.

"Probably."

And there she stood, naked and vulnerable.

He plunged both hands though his hair. "Tara..."

"What?"

She saw the torment on his face. It was the same torment that ran through her heated blood. This was a loss of control for both of them.

But she was willing, if even for a short time, to give in.

He obviously was not.

"I'll get out of your way."

"Clint—"

But he was already stalking past her. "Enjoy your bath."

Candles flickered and burned around her. Vanilla scented the room. Romance and sex and intensity lingered.

But hope had just closed the bathroom door on her. He'd tested himself, and won.

Enjoy your bath.

"I'll do my best," she whispered into the stillness, staring down at her discarded clothes.

Eight

Clint sat beside her bed, watching as the darkness of a winter night moved across her heart-shaped face, casting mysterious shadows on her full mouth and high cheekbones.

Dressed in a pale-green tank top and whatever the white sheet at her waist was hiding, Tara looked so beautiful, still a girl in so many ways—yet there was no denying she was all woman.

He'd seen the evidence of her luscious female form this morning, the candlelight in the bathroom illuminating every curve, every valley to gut-wrenching perfection.

Clint allowed himself one moment to recall the pale-pink creaminess of her skin, her small waist and round hips. And then there were her full breasts and thoroughly excited nipples. More than once today he'd imagined his mouth on her, his tongue lapping at those taut peaks, hearing her moan and sigh.

Just the thought had him hard as granite.

And he'd walked out on her. For what? To protect her? To protect himself from a need so strong it could barely be contained, a need he knew they'd both never experienced before?

A need that could ruin them both, lacerate the thin shield of control they both clung to?

The scar on his chest felt raw suddenly, and he curbed that line of thought, put all his focus back on the beauty before him.

Resisting the urge to inch closer, he sat back, crossing his arms over his chest. He had an insatiable need, a compulsion, to be near this woman. Not just for protection's sake or to fulfill an aching desire, but something more.

It was becoming all too clear that when Tara was near, when her eyes met his and her voice uttered his name, he changed into someone he barely recognized. He was a man, instead of the walking corpse he'd been for the past three years. He was alive. And no matter how alarming it was to feel that way, the sensation was too good to try to quell it.

Before him, her long blond curls splayed about the pillow, Tara shifted in her sleep. Then her eyelashes fluttered and lifted. Soft green pools stared up at him with no fear, only a bit of confusion. He cursed himself. He'd wanted to be out of the room before she woke up.

She stayed where she was, her voice soft and a bit husky as she said, "Morning."

"Not anymore it's not," he said with a subtle grin.

"What time is it?"

"Close to five."

"I slept too long." Startled, she started to sit up.

Clint eased her back against the pillows gently. "You're fine."

"I've wasted the day."

"You're right where you should be, Tara."

She looked cozy and sexy as hell, and Clint desperately wanted to rip back the covers and crawl in beside her, beneath her, atop her—anywhere that skin grazed skin.

"But you're not where you should be, are you?" She raised an amused brow at him as she stretched her arms over her head.

"Noticed that, did you?"

"I may be a little out of it, but that much I can tell."

"You're not out of it, Tara, you're probably still a little tired, that's all."

"It was the bath," she said wryly, her mouth curving into a wry smile. "Way too relaxing."

He couldn't help himself. He leaned down, whispered in her ear, "It had the opposite effect on me."

"Serves you right, Andover," she chided.

When he lifted his head a few inches, his mouth

hovered above her mouth. ''That wasn't about not wanting you, Tara.''

''No?''

''No. It was about wanting you too much.''

She nodded, took a deep breath, but Clint could clearly see in those liquid green eyes of hers that his departure had hurt her.

''So,'' she said lightly, ''is something wrong? Did Jane call?''

Sitting up again, Clint shook his head. ''Nothing's wrong. Jane did call. I guess she and Autumn and Marissa are making ornaments for the tree. She didn't want to leave, so I sent Harry over there for the night. Between him and Sorrenson, they don't need me.''

''So—''

He nodded. ''I'm staying here.''

''Right.'' In the fading twilight, he watched Tara's gaze flicker to the bedspread, then back up to him. ''So, Mr. Andover, if Jane's fine, why are you...'' She waved a hand in his direction.

''Why am I sitting beside your bed?''

She nodded.

''I suppose you wouldn't buy 'protection' as an excuse, would you?''

''Not really.''

''Well, the truth is, I had an idea.''

Her eyebrows shot up. ''About the case? Has there been a development?''

''No.''

''Then what is it?''

"It involves getting dressed and venturing outside."

She waited about ten seconds, then said, "That's all you're going to tell me, right?"

"That's it."

"You really live for suspense, don't you?"

"It's my business, sweetheart."

The ache that had settled in his groin as he'd watched her sleep earlier now moved up into his chest. He had a foolish tongue, one that was getting him into more and more trouble whenever he was around Tara.

He watched her intently, looking for a sign that she was affected by his rash endearment. She gave none.

Instead, she shooed him off the bed, muttering a terse, "All right. Give me a few minutes to get ready."

But as he walked out her bedroom door, he wasn't altogether sure whether he was relieved by the lack of response or disappointed.

Snow fell from the gray heavens above onto the flat grounds of Royal Park. But Tara didn't feel its soft, damp pursuit. Under the shelter of the gazebo, she sat beside Clint and gazed out at the terrific beauty of an early season snowfall.

It was a fusion of odd yet wonderful feelings, she thought. The warmth of the man next to her, the scent of snow and earth and male tickling her senses, the intense urge to place her hand in his and squeeze.

Years and years ago this park had housed two young lovers sharing their first kiss. Tonight they had returned.

But to what end, it remained to be seen.

She'd decided to be and act and respond as she wanted without reproach and control, regardless of what path Clint choose to travel. She wouldn't have regret with this situation, this man. Not this time. After this whole mess with Jane was cleared up, she could return to her real life. But until then she was free. And she wanted Clint.

It was up to him now whether he could take what she was offering or not.

"It was summer the last time I was here," Clint said, leaning back against one of the slender gazebo walls.

"I remember." Reclining with him, Tara smiled. "You really haven't been here since then?"

"No, you?"

She shook her head. "I thought someday when I had a family, I'd bring them here."

"Sure."

"Did you have the same thought?"

The minute the words were out of her mouth, Tara wanted to pull them back. How could she say something like that without thinking?

"I'm sorry, Clint, I—"

"It's no problem."

"It was insensitive."

"It's done."

Every ounce of the caregiver that dwelled inside of her wanted to comfort him, hold him as he told her what it was like to lose his wife, what it was like to have the promise of family ripped from you.

From the moment they'd gotten reacquainted, that day the Texas Cattleman's Club members had brought Jane to the hospital, Tara could sense that Clint still carried a heavy burden from losing his wife in that fire. Sure, he'd kept the pain hidden beneath a tough, almost mechanical, exterior. But she'd seen it. It was in her makeup to see beneath the surface of a person.

But she'd kept her questions, solutions and advice to herself. Back then she reasoned that Clint's past was none of her business, that he obviously had his own way of dealing with his grief and wasn't welcoming any comments.

Now, after all that they'd been through over the past several weeks, she wasn't so sure what was her business and what wasn't.

"You know," she said on a sigh. "I actually did come back here once more. Well, almost."

He glanced over at her. "Really?"

"Yep."

"And?"

"It was with another guy."

Clint pinned her with a devilish gaze. "And I thought this spot was sacred."

"It was," she insisted sweetly.

"Then how could you, Nurse Roberts?"

She laughed into the snowy silence. "I said I *almost* came here."

"Hmm." He frowned darkly. "So, who was the guy?"

"Ronnie Pemberton," she said, lifting her nose in the air. "College man."

"Sounds serious."

Tara sighed, remembering the ambitious young man and his desperate need for female attention—heck, any kind of attention had worked for him. "I thought it might be."

"And Ronnie?"

"He thought it was a spring-break-fling type of thing."

"Idiot."

"We were both kids."

"Even a kid should know a good thing when he sees it."

"You think so?"

On a weighty sigh, he took hold of her shoulders and turned her to face him. "Yes, I do."

Tara tried like heck to keep the mood light, but when he was this close she felt weak, pliant in his hands. "I wish you would've been around then."

"Why is that?" he asked, one hand raking up her shoulder, over her collarbone as his eyes went stormy.

She shivered, but not from the cold—from the impact of his gaze. "You could have given Ronnie a good talking to."

"I'm not much of a talker." His palm cupped her neck, his fingers threading in her hair. "I would've given him a good beating instead."

"He was a black belt," she uttered breathlessly as he moved toward her, his gaze on her mouth.

"He was an idiot."

And then he lowered his head and covered her mouth with his. Tara's eyes fell closed, but her heart burst open like a dam that had held its water back for thousands of years. He tasted so good, so right. And the way he touched her, the way his fingers plunged into her hair as he pulled her closer, deepening their kiss, it was pure magic.

The blast of pleasure he created within her moved from moment to moment. It began as a tingling in her mouth, then dropped to her breasts and finally dove into her womb, where it ached and yearned.

And when his mouth parted, when his tongue gently lapped at her lower lip, she moaned her need. Her hands to his face, she played with him, slid her tongue over his, nibbled at his lips.

"We're repeating history," she whispered against his mouth.

"No," he growled, inching back just a bit so he could look in her eyes. "This is altogether different...."

The sound of approaching laughter cut into their little world, made them ease apart. Out of the corner of her eye, Tara saw a family coming toward them. Two kids, two parents, having a grand old time in the snow.

"How about a walk by the lake?" she suggested, turning back to face him.

Clint raised an eyebrow. "Looking for an escort, ma'am?"

She grinned. "Something like that."

"Well, a man's got to do what a man's got to do, I suppose." He stood.

She sighed, rolled her eyes. "What a gentleman."

"I'd never make that claim, ma'am."

With a wry grin, he took her hand in his large warm one, helped her to her feet and led her down the gazebo steps.

"Well, I think it's only fair."

Clint took a last bite of artichoke pasta, then reached for his glass of wine. "What's that?"

From across the smallish dining table in her warm and very comfortable living room, Tara looked up at him and smiled. "You made breakfast, so I made dinner."

"Yep, that does sound fair."

She nodded, reached for her own glass of merlot.

"A damn fine dinner, too, by the way," he said, giving her a broad grin.

"Thank you."

It was late, for supper at any rate. Going on nine o'clock. But neither of them seemed to notice much. For Clint a home-cooked meal made and shared with a woman he found near to irresistible was a rarity, and he wasn't too proud to admit he didn't want the night to end.

"You're deep in thought."

Her observation nudged him from those thoughts, had him searching for what to say. "Just trying to remember the last time I had a home-cooked meal."

"Come up with anything?"

He shook his head. "It's been a while."

"Well, you're always welcome here."

He shot her a sidelong glance. "Am I?"

"Yes, of course," she said quickly. Then awkwardly she cleared her throat. "It's just that I love to cook, and food should be shared."

"I couldn't agree more."

She cocked her head to the side, studied him. "Are you making fun of me, Andover? Because I still have some marinara sauce left." With her wineglass, she gestured toward his white shirt. "Red and white go great together."

He chuckled. "I'm not making fun. I swear it." He drank deeply from his glass. "In fact, I pinky swear."

Her eyes widened and she gasped dramatically. "I haven't made a pinky swear in fifteen years."

"Then it's about time don't you think?" Clint said, leaning in, offering her his pinky.

She tossed him a withering glance, but her smile was bright and playful as she, too, leaned in and wrapped her pinky around his.

A few more inches and he could taste that sweet mouth of hers again. Or better yet, maybe he'd just push aside this table and haul her onto his lap.

His gaze moved over her face, her eyes, her mouth. "So, best dish you make?"

"Hmm," she began, tugging on her lower lip with her teeth as she thought. "Stuffed cabbage, I'd say. My grandmother's recipe."

"Sounds good."

"It is."

"But…"

"But?" Her finger tightened around his.

"How many other men have you made this stuffed cabbage for?"

"Does it matter?"

Clint paused for a moment, his brain suddenly fuzzy. He'd begun this whole line of questions in jest. What the hell had happened? Did it really matter that she'd made some dish for some other guy?

Yes, it did.

Silently cursing himself, he said aloud, "Just wondering, is all. So, how many is it?"

Her manner still playful, she furrowed her brow and started counting her fingers. But the more she did, the more annoyed Clint got.

What a fool, he thought.

When she finally turned back to him, she wore a great big smile. "Zero."

It took a moment for Clint to get the joke. And when he did, he released his hold on her pinky and sat back in his chair, took another swallow of wine. "Farce doesn't suit you, Roberts."

Tara laughed, shook her head. "And jealousy doesn't suit you, Andover."

"This has nothing to do with jealousy."

"No? Then what is it?"

"Well, it's certainly not jealously." He snorted derisively. "We're just playing around here."

Her face fell and her eyes lost their luster. "Right." She stood up, gathered some plates and headed into the kitchen. "I forgot."

He wanted to kick himself. "Tara."

"I can get this all cleaned up. You must have work to do or something."

"You know I'm not going anywhere."

She stopped what she was doing, eyed him curiously. "Why is that? You still have a man guarding my house, right?"

"Right."

"So there's really no reason for you to be here."

"Maybe I want to finish what we started this morning." He stood up beside her, cupped her face, ran his thumb over her mouth. "What we started in the gazebo."

Her eyes flashed fire. "Maybe you do, but I doubt that you will."

"What the hell does that mean?" he barked.

"You know very well."

Fury gripped his chest. "What do you want me to say, Tara?" On something close to a growl, he raked a hand through his hair. "That this, whatever it is between us, is real? That I can give you more than I'm capable of? Or that I'm jealous as hell even thinking about you giving anything, even a stupid cabbage dish, to another man?"

"Only if it's true."

"This is what's true." He lowered his mouth to hers, gave her a long, drugging kiss. "And this," he uttered, his mouth once again closing in. "And this." Hunger drenched his kiss, and Clint felt her shudder in his hands. "And this."

Anger flooded him. Anger at himself and at her for making him this crazy. But he used that passion as he made love to her mouth.

She tasted so good. Like wine and need and want. And when she ran her hands up his shoulders, wrapped them around his neck, he reveled in the power of pulling her closer, of having her in his arms.

How could anyone fit so well? he wondered. Her breasts to his chest, the curve of her hips to his aching groin. Pure perfection.

Wasting no more time on thought, he found her neck, felt her pulse beating rapidly against his lips, urging him on—urging him to take what he'd only fantasized about taking.

And he followed the call, trailing hot, sensual kisses down her neck.

To Clint's satisfaction, Tara let her head fall back, let a moan escape her throat. Her surrender and her obvious desire had Clint mad with longing and hard as steel. He wanted to take her fast, feel every inch of her at once. But he held himself in check. With her, he would take his time.

Slowly he moved down her collarbone, grazing his teeth over her skin as he went, smiling as she bucked her hips against him with each nibble.

"Tara." Groaning at the desperation he felt to consume her, Clint pulled back, took her face in his hands.

"I don't know what you think about this, about me, but what I'm about to say is the truth."

Her eyes opened slowly. She looked drugged. "Tell me."

"I'm not playing here."

Her cheeks were flushed, her mouth pink, and those green eyes glowed smoky heat. "I know."

"You don't know," he argued as much to himself as to her. "This isn't some innocent flirtation or the culmination of too much highly charged banter."

Astonishment touched her flushed face.

He leaned in, brushed his lips over hers. "I want you, Tara, in a way that scares me. And I can't control it any longer."

"Clint…"

"I need you to tell me to back off and get out of here right now if you don't want this. If you don't want me."

Tara felt as if her heart would burst at his words. If she didn't want him? Was he serious? Hadn't he noticed that she was falling hopelessly for him? Hadn't he seen the way her body responded to his touch, his kiss, every time they were close?

For twenty years she'd given all she had in the name of propriety, of what was right. She'd held herself in check, done what was expected. It was high time she let the gates come crashing down. Even if they had to be rebuilt later.

Lord, did she want him?

Her gaze locked to his, she took his hands and placed

them on the hem of her sweater. Then she lifted her arms. "Let's try this again."

His eyes went blue-black as he stared at her. Then he moved, lifting the fabric over her head in one wicked swoosh. As soon as she was free of her sweater, he took her mouth again, kissing her breathless as he eased off her cotton bra.

She stood before him, nude from the waist up, vulnerable as a kitten, waiting for him to touch her, needing him to touch her, praying he wouldn't leave her standing alone again.

But he didn't leave her.

He stroked her.

Reaching out, he took her breasts in his hands, possessively at first, making her womb tighten and ache as he kneaded her flesh. Then he eased back, his palms lightly brushing the tips of her breasts as his thumbs stroked her nipples. Tara moaned with desire and pressed back into his large, strong hands. Her skin felt tight and hot, her body anxious for more.

And Clint gave. He raked his hands down her torso, gently caressing her belly, then fiercely gripping her waist. The feeling of being possessed nearly had her legs buckling beneath her. But she held steady.

That is, until his head lowered and his mouth closed in.

Tara cried out as his wet, hot tongue met the swollen crest of her breast. The sensation was like magic, only, a magic she'd never experienced. Fire shot straight down into her core and stayed there, rolling and churning as Clint suckled her hardened nipple.

Her mind dimmed, her senses peaked, she ran a hand up his denim-clad thigh until she found what she wanted.

Clint groaned, tipped his head back as she palmed him. He was hard and ready, and so was she.

"I want you inside me," she said breathlessly.

"Now?"

"Now! No more waiting."

"Then hold on."

In one swift move, he lifted her into his arms and carried her down the hall and into her dark bedroom, kissing her as he went.

They bumped into a wall or two, but it mattered little. They were together, they were making love, and the feeling was pure bliss.

Tara reveled in the feeling of this man she was falling in love with. Clint made her feel alive, in touch with herself and the true desires of her heart—all that she'd wanted but denied herself.

When they reached the edge of the bed, they dropped onto the mattress, their mouths still entwined, their tongues warring for more pleasure.

Outside, the snow fell to the ground in perfect silence. So unlike what was happening inside.

Clothing was being torn off, skin was being nibbled, the sound of a condom packet being ripped open mingled with the sounds of desperation and desire erupting from Tara's throat.

Years of wondering what this man would feel like atop her, his scent fusing with hers, the delicious weight of his body pressing down into hers.

He was here now. And she felt so lucky.

But she wanted to see him, all of him—watch his eyes turn black as she stroked him, as he pushed inside of her body.

She reached for the lamp, but, poised above her, Clint caught her wrist.

"No."

"Why?"

He cursed raggedly. "I don't want you to see me."

"I don't care about your scar, Clint—"

"I care."

Disregarding his dark tone, Tara reached up, tried to touch his chest, but Clint stopped her.

"Please, Tara."

"All right," she said, acquiescing, knowing she could never understand the pain that drove him to feel this kind of shame. And she didn't want to inflict more.

"Thank you."

He released her hand, kissed her softly, sensually, and she wrapped her arms around him. She didn't need to see. She would feel him, his wounded chest, this way, against her skin, the only way she could.

As his kiss grew wild, desperate, his hands moved, stroking her skin, whispering erotic phrases into her heated mouth.

The words made the urgency inside her soar to a dangerous level, and she pressed her hips up, needing to feel his erection, his steely need for her, against her belly.

"Wrap your legs around me, Tara," he commanded, reaching underneath her and lifting her hips.

Anxious to get closer, she slid her legs out from under him and around his waist, pressing the wet core of herself against him.

His gaze locked to hers, he raised up and eased down inside of her with one long stroke.

Tara cried out, the feeling so electric she nearly lost her breath.

But she didn't lose her instinct, her need.

She bucked against him, and he rose up, then drove into her. Over and over. Pumping inside her as she stretched for him, met him—each stroke a perfect arrow to her heart, to her very soul.

Tara could barely hold on. The waves of climax were close, threatening to crash against the white-hot sand of her core.

But control had no place here.

And that was quickly proven when Clint thrust deep inside her, then dipped his head and took her nipple deep into his mouth.

Rolls of sweet ecstasy overtook her, and she cried out, moaning and moving and gripping his back with her nails as she clenched around him, welcoming every shudder that ripped through her body.

"No games," Clint uttered hoarsely, then reared back and took his own pleasure.

Nine

——

The nightmare hadn't come.

Clint scrubbed a hand over his eyes, then glanced at the bedside clock. Illuminated in the dingy sunrise, he saw that it was barely seven o'clock in the morning.

He let his head fall back against the pillows. For the first time in three years, he'd slept straight through the night without incident.

The implications of that fact rolled through him, made his chest tighten.

Last night. And Tara.

He inhaled deeply. He didn't want to need anyone, rely on anyone to get through the night. Even her.

Turning his head toward the window, Clint stared at

the freedom of the outdoors. Snow glistened on the ground, while overhead, clouds covered the sky. There would be another day of cold and snow.

A perfect day for hibernating.

But staying beneath the covers wasn't an option for him, couldn't be, no matter how great it sounded. He had to get up, out of bed and head over to the Sorrensons' to check on Jane, then go on over to his office. He had an investigation to see to, problems to solve, a mystery to uncover.

Beside him Tara stirred, her smooth, toned back arching, while her silky bottom brushed his thigh. He was reminded of last night. How she'd responded to his every touch, how she'd trusted him enough to give him the shelter of the darkness.

How soft her inner thighs had felt when he eased them apart and slid inside her.

Clint turned toward her, his arm curling around her waist, easing her back and tucking her into the hollow of his body.

The warmth of her was addicting, as was the sweet, vanilla scent of her hair that tickled his nose. He hadn't let a woman get this close to him since...well, in a long time. It wasn't that he'd been a monk in the past three years. But his affairs had been short-lived, a mutually enjoyable experience with no ties.

But with Tara everything was different. He wanted more than a physical release with her, from her, and that want shamed him.

When had needing this woman, this high school infatuation, happened? How had he allowed it?

And, he wondered, running his hand over the smooth surface of her belly, would he abandon all sense and duty and allow it to happen again?

"Hmm," she mumbled. "Feels good."

Damn right it did.

"What time is it?" she asked, her voice husky with sleep.

"It's early. Close to seven."

"Why are you up?"

"What a choice of words, Nurse Roberts."

She laughed softly, arched her back and pressed her bottom against his shaft. "You know what I mean. Is something wrong?"

"Not a thing." If he kept his mind and reason at bay, that statement might actually be true.

"Having regrets, Andover?"

Her voice was laced with teasing, but Clint could hear the underlying thread of unease there. Maybe because he, too, wondered if there were any regrets on her part.

He wouldn't ask, though. He didn't want to know.

"Are you kidding?" he said, his hands raking up her belly, cupping her breasts, warm and soft and full.

She sucked in a breath. "Just want to make sure, that's all."

He nuzzled her neck, told her the truth, whispered it against her skin. "The only thing I regret is having to get out of this bed, get in my cold car and head to my cold office.''

"So wait until it warms up a little.''

"When do you think that'll be?''

She took his hand, trailed it down her torso, placed it over the soft curls at the juncture of her thighs. "Anytime now.''

Clint groaned at the unexpected, but completely sensual action. "Close your eyes,'' he commanded. "And keep them closed.''

"Why?''

"It's a surprise.''

"A good one?'' she asked, the smile evident in her voice.

In two seconds he had her on her back. "You won't be sorry, I promise you.''

She didn't ply him with any more questions. She did as he ordered. Her eyes closed, lips parted in anticipation, she looked ready and willing and so trusting of him he nearly leaned down and whispered for her to look at him, the real him, the scarred him.

But he wouldn't allow himself to be that exposed.

Instead he stripped back the covers and eased himself over her. For a moment, he just looked, took in the sweetness of her. So beautiful, so full of life. Then he glanced down at the swollen flesh between her thighs and growled.

So wet.

Since the moment he'd peeled off her clothes that

first time in the candlelit bathroom, he'd wanted this, wanted to bury himself between her thighs, taste her.

He heard Tara release a soft whimper as he lowered his head to her belly, then a moan as he touched his mouth to her skin. His own breathing ragged, he placed his hands on her thighs and coaxed her legs wide apart as he trailed his tongue down the smooth softness of her stomach.

She bucked, lifting her hips, trying to get closer as she whimpered again and again, showing him what she wanted and where she wanted it. And Clint, his brain given over to desire, his body rock hard and ready, could only do as she wished.

But he would go slowly with her pleasure, he thought as he ran his tongue lightly over the hot, swollen length of her femininity.

A cry of such intense pleasure erupted from Tara's throat that it nearly undid him. But he battled on. Like a starving man, he stroked her with his tongue, nibbled, suckled, covered her completely as he tasted heaven.

He tried for a slow rise, a slow and steady path to climax. But it was not as her body intended. She was close, ready to take as her thighs shook around him.

And when he felt her body stiffen, he brought his hand up between her legs and plunged two fingers inside of her as he continued to work her over and over, stroke by stroke with his mouth.

Her shudders of climax surrounded him, her cries, her calls of his name, made him mad with desire. And when she held her arms out for him, he rose up, and after quickly slipping on a condom, pushed inside her body.

His thrusts were as wild and wicked as his tongue had been, and he watched as Tara moved with him, her head thrashing from side to side, moaning is if she never wanted him to stop. But still she kept her eyes closed.

The tender gesture undid him, made him feel cared for, cherished, for the first time in a long time.

He wanted this woman so desperately it ached. But he had nothing to offer, nothing but a past and a pain that haunted him, followed him everywhere he went.

Tara deserved more. She deserved a whole man, not a man with a charred heart.

But this morning as she bucked and moaned beneath him, as he slammed into the hot, loving glove of her body, as he felt her shuddering with completion once again, he gave up that idealism.

And gave in to his own climax.

"Ohmigod!"

The clearly feminine curse from the living room woke Tara with a start. Bleary-eyed and stiff, she sat up and looked around, tried to get her bearings.

"What was that?" she whispered as much to herself as to a sleeping Clint.

"I think it was Jane."

Tara whirled around to face the man in her bed, clutching the sheet to her chest. "She's home."

"It would appear so."

"Hey, Andover?" This time a male voice, low and purposeful boomed through the house. "You in here?"

Clint rested on his side, propped up on one elbow, his chest, and the scar it held, obscured by pillows. "It would also appear that David Sorrenson brought her home."

"You're awfully calm about this."

"And you're entirely too agitated." He gave her a slow, seductive smile. "Come on. Lie back down."

"And what? They'll just think we're not here and go away?"

"One can hope."

"Tara?" Jane called agitatedly. "Tara? Please. Are you here?"

"I'll be right there, Jane." Tara slipped out of bed, reached for her thick terry cloth robe. Then she glanced over at Clint. "Something's wrong, I can tell. Are you coming?"

He nodded, his eyes serious now, as he'd heard the anxious tone of Jane's voice, too. "I'll be right behind you."

Without waiting, Tara hurried out of the room and down the hall. She saw Jane right away, sitting at the dining table Tara had shared with Clint last night. Jane looked terrified.

Tara went to her, put an arm around her shoulders. "What's wrong? Are you okay?"

"No," she began, then shook her head. "I mean…it's this." She held up a piece of paper. "This letter…"

A pang of fear coursed through Tara as she stared at the cream-colored scrap of paper in Jane's shaky hand. Another letter. And this time Jane had found it.

"It was stuck in the door when we got here," David informed her from his spot by the door. "It was addressed to Jane, so—"

"I thought it was a note from you guys." Jane looked at Tara, then past her.

Tara glanced over her shoulder. Clint stood not five feet away, fully dressed, his blue eyes icy and ready to pounce.

Settling back against the door, David crossed his arms over his wide chest. "Sorry to interrupt, pal, but—"

Clint made a dismissive gesture with his hand. "Never mind that. Are you telling me this letter was stuck in the door, not in the mailbox?"

David nodded. "No stamp, no return address, no nothing."

"Just my name on the front of the envelope," Jane added.

Teeth clenched, Clint muttered, "How the hell did that bastard get past my man?"

"The letter says Autumn isn't mine." Shaking her head, Jane said, "I don't understand this. I feel that I should, but I don't."

Attempting to soothe her friend, Tara placed her hand over Jane's. "It's okay. Don't push yourself or put too much pressure on yourself over something you can't control."

On a curse Clint stalked over to Jane, held out his hand. "Can I see that?"

With a shaky nod, Jane handed him the letter. Tara rose to her feet and read over his shoulder. The boldly typed words were chilling.

You have taken the child.
You are a thief and a liar.
You will get what you deserve.
No one can protect you now.

Clint glanced up, raised a brow at David. "This is pretty damn bold, don't you think?"

"He has no fear," David remarked.

"Well, that's a big mistake."

Tara sighed. "Whoever it is doesn't feel they need to hide behind the U.S. Post Office anymore or concern themselves with your guards."

"Typical behavior for a psychopath," Clint said, holding the paper to the light. "The increase in frequency and the blatant disregard for his victim's personal space."

David cleared his throat. "I think we should consider moving Jane."

Tara inched closer to Jane. "Won't this person be watching? I mean, should we act scared? Act like we're running or panicking?"

"We should act smart, Tara," Clint said, his lips thinning.

"Of course we should," she tossed back. "I'm not saying—"

"You need to stop being so stubborn and think about Jane's welfare."

"Back to the same old argument, are we?" Hands on her hips, Tara narrowed her eyes. "Call me whatever you will, Andover, but I *am* thinking about Jane's welfare. Moving her right now is a mistake."

He raised a brow. "Is this about her being at my place? Or me not being here?"

Tara sucked in a breath, feeling as though she'd just been punched in the gut. "I'd tell you to get out, but I don't think your head will fit through the door."

"Stop this!"

Tara and Clint turned to look at Jane.

"We'll decide where I belong in a minute. But first, I have a question." A new strength now resided in her violet eyes. "Have there been other letters?"

Tara looked at Clint. Jaw tight, he nodded at Jane.

"How many?" she asked.

"Two others."

"And you didn't tell me? Neither one of you thought this was any of my business?"

"We thought it was best, Jane," Tara explained, guilt seeping into her pores. "We didn't want to upset you. But that was wrong. You had a right to know what was happening, and we're sorry."

The pretty brunette nodded, "Thank you for that." Then she released a weighty breath and asked, "Well, what do we do now?"

This time when Clint spoke, his voice lacked any anger or frustration. He was calm and cool and all business. "David, you take the ladies over to your place and—"

Tara shook her head. "Clint, I won't be chased out of my house by some lunatic—"

"Tara," Clint caught her gaze, and his deep, blue eyes reminded her this was the man she had just made love with who was asking her to forget their stupid argument and trust him. "This one time, don't fight me, okay?"

Her heart squeezed, and she released her own anger and found the sensibility in his request. "All right. But I'll drive myself. I have to work tonight."

"Maybe you should get someone to cover—"

"Clint..."

He nodded. "All right." Then he turned to David. "We need to move on this."

"I'll take care of everything," David said. "No problem."

Grabbing his coat and keys, Clint headed for the door. "I'll see you later."

Tara couldn't help but call out, ask him, "Where are you going now?"

"While David takes you back to the ranch, I'm taking this letter in myself and making some phone calls."

Moving close to Tara and Jane, David said, "Meeting in two hours?"

Clint nodded, then turned to Tara. "I promised I'd take care of this and I will."

"I know." She managed a small, tentative smile. "Be careful."

Though his eyes remained stern, he flashed her a tight grin of his own. "You, too."

The men of the Texas Cattleman's Club sat in overstuffed leather chairs in the quiet shadows of the Cattleman's Club cigar lounge. As they nursed a rare Scotch in four heavy crystal glasses, they spoke in low tones, leaving all the action in the room to the wait staff and bartender, who were trading stories with several members sitting at the ornate bar.

"Clearly we're being strung along," Alex announced with quiet force.

"And we seem to be eagerly following the breadcrumbs," David added, his tone dry.

Ryan agreed, his dark gaze shifting to Clint. "What did your man have to say on the subject?"

Clint sighed heavily. "He assured me that there was an eye on that house every moment."

"Then how does he explain how the letter got there?"

"He can't."

A grim line formed between Alex's eyebrows. "So where do we stand at present?"

Frustration arced through Clint. "More and intensive testing on this last letter."

"But you don't think they'll find anything, do you?" Ryan asked tightly, before taking a healthy swallow of Scotch.

Clint shook his head. "Whoever this guy is, he's sharp, quick and hard to catch."

Earlier, at the lab, Clint had closeted himself in one of the sterile rooms and given it everything he had. Forgoing any help this time, he'd done the work-up on the letter himself. He'd looked for things that no one would think necessary to look for. He'd tested for traces of fiber, bodily fluids, even had a rush on DNA.

But nothing had shown up.

And he could barely contain his anger and contrition at his failure to find one damn clue.

"Well—" David finished his drink, then leaned back in his leather chair and sighed "—looks like we're in for a fight."

"I'm all for a good fight." Ryan's brown eyes flashed. "Just like roping a reluctant steer."

Alex chuckled. "Still haven't gotten that life out of your system, have you?"

"Shut up, Kent."

"All right, boys," David interrupted with a patient grin. "Let's get back on track here."

"We need a next move," Clint said, eyeing each man in the dim light of the lounge, looking for suggestions.

David spoke first. "I think the main thing is to get both of the women out of that house."

"I agree," Clint said.

The argument he'd had with Tara that morning ran through his mind like ice water. He'd said some pretty stupid things, childish, insecure things—things a man who feels he might lose something that's precious to him might say. Tonight he would apologize, maybe even admit that it was really his wish that she stay close to him.

"Who's guarding them now?" Ryan asked.

"My buddy down at the police department is there with them," Clint replied.

"Where should they go?" Alex said, his eyebrows raised. "They could stay where they are, at Sorrensons' place."

David placed his glass on the table and nodded. "We've got plenty of room."

It wasn't a bad suggestion. Actually, it was the most sensible one. But Clint just couldn't agree to it. He'd vowed to protect Jane and Tara at all costs, and that was just what he intended to do.

"I'm taking them to my place," he informed the men, over the sudden rush of Club members converging on the lounge. "It can be locked up tighter than a fort if need be."

"Tara might give you trouble," David guessed.

She was already giving him trouble, Clint mused with a wry grin. With her stubborn nature, and in ways he couldn't even admit to himself much less share with his buddies.

"She'll go," he said with more confidence than he felt. "Even if I have to carry her out of the house kicking and screaming."

David chuckled. "Sounds interesting."

"Sounds dangerous," Ryan added, wiggling his eyebrows.

Alex slapped his friend on the back and said, "Sounds like trouble."

"You have no idea how much trouble," Clint said, giving each man a grim smile. "I'm guessing that right about now she's getting frustrated and bored, and she's roping the girls into ditching my cop buddy and going out somewhere."

"She wouldn't," Alex said, surprised.

"Oh, yes, she would." Clint shook his head. "And damned if her unbridled ways aren't part of the reason I'm crazy about her."

Ten

The bitch would be his.

Impatience snaked through his blood as he leaned forward in his office chair and reached for his tumbler of whiskey. Having what he wanted, what he'd come here for, was going to take more time.

Granted, he wasn't fond of waiting, but he had little choice in the matter. He hadn't counted on this town, this group of cowboys, protecting his prize the way they were.

But then again, they hadn't counted on him.

The nurse was getting restless and scared. Andover had come up with nothing, he was sure. The cowboy had been so consumed with bedding his blond nurse, he'd left his guards on for too long. The poor fool had gotten tired, fallen asleep for a minute or two.

Didn't Andover know that a minute was all the devil needed to do his handiwork? Or, he grinned broadly, to send in one of his fallen angels to do it for him.

Draining his glass of the stiff amber liquid, he picked up the phone and stabbed in the numbers. He had one more hand to deal out to the nurse and her lover, and it was about time he played it.

"Are we ready?" he barked into the receiver.

Jason Stokes's voice quivered nervously on the line. "Everything's set, boss."

"I hope so, for your sake."

"But like I said before, sir, if someone happens to be home...they could end up dead."

"I don't give a damn," the man snarled, growing weary of this subject. "The only thing I care about is getting my money. *How* it's done, doesn't concern me. Are we clear?"

"Yes, sir," Jason replied weakly.

"Good. Then see to it."

He didn't wait for a reply, didn't need one. He knew Stokes understood what would happen if he didn't get the job done. Hell, the bruises had barely healed from the last time the fool had disobeyed an order.

Standing up, he stalked over to his office window and stared out at Royal, Texas. God, he had to get out of this silly little town. But when he did, he was going to make sure he left with a renewed sense of pride, revenge against the woman that had stolen from him and the two packages he'd come for...

That baby and his half million dollars.

Eleven

"**W**as I right?" Pointing to a particularly beautiful Christmas tree on the large and very festively dressed lot, Tara looked expectantly at Jane and Marissa. "Or was I right?"

Marissa grinned, displaying the dimple in her right cheek. "I'd say you were right."

"I swear, just the scent of it cheers a person up, doesn't it?" Tara asked whimsically.

Jane nodded, hugging a little bundled-up Autumn to her chest. "It's beautiful."

"Do you think it's too tall for my living room?"

Jane shook her head. "Not at all."

Marissa snorted into the cold late-afternoon air.

"You should see the size of the one David brought home the other day. He called it my first of many presents. And honest to God, it looked like it had been sitting in some Oregon forest for thirty years."

"But you love it," Tara chided.

"Of course," Marissa agreed.

"Ah, the pampering of the newly married."

"You could have it all, too, Tara," she said thoughtfully.

Jane laughed. "Well, first she has to admit she's in love."

A soft gasp escaped Tara's throat. Not from hearing her own thoughts spoken aloud for the first time, but from realizing that the others around her saw what was in her heart. How could she, the sensible and oh-so-private Nurse Roberts, have allowed herself to be so exposed?

She touched her face, wondering for a moment if the adolescent notebook scribbling "I love Clint Andover" was written across it in red letters.

As one of the young men working the tree lot stalked past them, a measuring stick in his hand, Marissa leaned close and whispered, "David told me about your overnight guest."

Tara could feel her cheeks turning red—and it had nothing to do with the cold. "David has a big mouth."

Marissa wiggled her eyebrows. "All the better to kiss me with, my dear."

Her luminous violet eyes twinkling with amusement,

Jane broke out into laughter. So did Marissa, and Tara was quick to follow.

It had been a long time since she'd felt the intimacy of friendship. Sure, she adored the other nurses at the hospital, thought of them as family, but this was somehow different. Soft, silly banter about boys, girlish laughter…it was something she'd missed out on in school. And something she was so thankful she had now—even if it meant having her emotions unveiled.

"Hey, look," Marissa exclaimed. "Santa's here." She touched Jane's hand. "Do you mind if I take Autumn over to see him?"

"Of course not," Jane replied as she eased the wide-eyed baby into her aunt Marissa's waiting arms.

Lovingly, Marissa carried her off toward the gathering crowd, leaving Tara and Jane alone. For the first time that day, Tara noticed the same thread of anxiety that had shadowed her friend's eyes this morning when she'd found the third scrap of hate mail.

Taking a seat on a nearby bench, Tara asked, "You can't stop thinking about the letter, can you?"

Jane shook her head. "I wish you'd told me about the others."

"I know, and I'm so sorry about that. We just thought the last thing you needed was to have another thing to worry about."

"I know." Jane sat down beside Tara on the bench, her violet eyes distressed.

"Everything's going to be okay," Tara assured her, though she wasn't altogether assured herself.

"Do you think Autumn is safe?"

"At David and Marissa's?"

"In general. Or do you think this maniac won't stop until he gets what he wants?"

"I don't know." It was an honest answer, but not the only one she had. "But what I do know is that Clint and David and the rest of the Texas Cattleman's Club won't give up until they catch this guy."

Jane nodded firmly, but her fears clearly weren't allayed.

"The TCC is an incredible group of men," Tara said. "They'll get to the bottom of this, I promise you."

"If I could just remember something." She shook her head. "It might help."

Tara eased a strand of her friend's long, dark hair away from her face, tucking it behind her ear. "Your memory will come back soon. Just give it time."

"But what if I'm running out of time, Tara?"

The moments seemed to slow as the two women looked at each other, both searching for answers they weren't sure would ever come.

Several yards away, parked at the Santa Station, Marissa called over to them, waving her free arm frantically. "She's up next. She's going to sit on Santa's lap, you guys. C'mon."

A sudden smile lit Jane's eyes and she stood up. "This I gotta see."

"Me, too," Tara agreed.

As they walked toward the Santa Station and all the

excited kids and proud parents, Jane said, "I'm going to stay with Autumn again tonight, if you don't mind."

"Oh, Jane, of course I don't mind. I totally understand."

"I wish you'd change your mind about going back home after your shift."

Tara frowned playfully. "I've got to drop off this tree somewhere, don't I?"

"Tara…"

All afternoon she'd thought about the letters and her home and the safety of all of them. Her mind was as heavy as her heart. What was wise? What was right?

"I worked my butt off to keep that house and fix it up," Tara said, "and I really feel I should stay there." She laughed a little sadly. "My mom would tan my hide if I ran away over a few threats."

Jane sighed heavily. "Clint's not going to like it, Tara."

"I can't worry about what Clint likes and doesn't like. Just as long as you and Autumn are safe. That's what matters."

"I'll be fine. And nothing and nobody will ever harm my child—not while I'm around. I'll do anything to make sure she'll be safe."

The determination in Jane's tone squeezed at Tara's heart as they neared the Santa Station. "I can't even begin to imagine the intense bond between a mother and her child."

Jane took her hand and led her to the front of the line where Autumn was cooing in the very round and jolly Santa's arms. "Like Marissa said, maybe some-day you'll find out."

"Maybe."

And for the first time in Tara's life, she wondered if such a lovely idea might actually be possible.

It was close to two-thirty in the morning when the headlights hit the window.

His jaw tight as a trap, Clint sat in Tara's pine-scented living room, without one lamp on. Gaze pinned to the door, he waited as those headlights switched off, as her feminine footfalls made their way up the drive-way and front stoop, as a key turned in the lock.

The hall light came on with a click, and Tara stood there in her nurse's scrubs, her blond tendrils falling around her face—a face that held a very alarmed ex-pression.

Until she recognized him.

Shaking her head, she fairly stuttered, "Jeez, An-dover…you scared me."

"Did I?"

"You're sitting here in the dark like some kind of—" She stopped short, took a breath.

"Some kind of what?"

She ignored the question, just shut the front door and walked into the living room. "So, what are you doing here? Guarding my tree?"

It was a lame joke and Clint didn't crack a smile. "You have no respect for authority, do you?"

She dropped her bag on the table. "Sure I do. When the request is reasonable."

"And I'm making unreasonable requests?"

Sitting down on the couch opposite him, she lifted her hands in the air. "We went out to get a tree, in a very public setting. It was no big deal."

She made him crazy. Not just his body, but his mind, as well. Whatever she claimed to be in the past, in the present she had no sense, only stubbornness. "It's not the tree, Tara. It's you, here, alone. For chrissakes, you just came home to an empty house. Anyone could've been here waiting for you—"

"You're waiting here."

Through gritted teeth he muttered, "I give up. You're impossible."

"Clint, the guy with the letters isn't after me."

"Perps like that don't give a damn about details. They just act—foolishly most of the time."

"The letters were all about Jane, not—"

He jumped to his feet. "Why can't you just trust me? Is that so hard for you to do?"

"Yes." Her tone was impassioned as her gaze raged green fire.

"Why?"

She didn't look away but she said nothing, and he wanted to grab her and shake her. His patience was thin tonight. After working his butt off to find something about the bastard who was after Jane and Autumn, and coming up with nothing, he wasn't willing to let Tara off the hook this time. He needed answers from someone today.

It took one stride to get to the couch. He took her hand and tugged her to her feet and within inches from him. "Why, Tara? Because relying on someone, trusting someone, is dangerous? Because it's a loss of control, what?"

She tipped her chin up a fraction. "Speaking from your own experience, Andover?"

"Maybe…maybe that's why it's so easy for me to see it in you," he replied boldly.

She shook her head, her eyes blazing with frustration. "Like you, control is all I have."

"That's nuts."

"No, it's survival. Always has been."

He understood all that she was saying. Her words had been his own, his mantra, so many times he couldn't count. So what the hell was he doing pushing her to give that up? If he accepted that attitude, used that attitude in his own life, why wasn't he able to accept it from her?

"I don't think you have as much control over yourself as you think, Tara," he said, easing a hand to the back of her neck, soft as silk.

"What do you mean?

"No chaperone again tonight. You let Jane stay at the Sorrensons'."

"She's safe at David and Marissa's, right?"

"Yes. She's safe."

"But?"

His palm tightened on the back of her neck. "But maybe you're not."

"With you here to protect me—"

"That's not the only reason why I'm here."

"No?"

He shook his head as he slid his knee between her thighs.

She snaked in a breath. "Are you here because you want to be with me?"

"All the time I want to be with you," he growled, dipped his forehead against hers. "I'm going insane with the need I feel for you."

Despite her weariness after working a full shift at the hospital, Tara felt a surge of heat in her belly. It was no surprise, this reaction to him, looking like he was all dressed in black, his shirt open at the collar.

And then there was the closeness, his scent and his touch.

She watched his lips move. "If something happened to you, I don't know…"

"Nothing's going to happen to me," Tara insisted. That slight shadow around his lips…she needed to feel him. "You're here."

Lifting her chin, she kissed his mouth. A groan escaped his lips, and he slipped an arm around her waist and pulled her to him. His chest crushed her, made her breasts tight and achy as he covered her mouth, returning her kiss with hot, hungry ones of his own.

The emotion inside of her exploded as she nibbled and stroked his bottom lip with her tongue. She imagined coming home every night to find him there, waiting for her, kissing her hello, then carrying her off to their bed.

Their bed.

She was mad.

Their bed.

She couldn't think of such things—hope and plan for something that was certain to end up being just a few wonderful nights of lovemaking, when all was said and done.

She eased back from him a little, just a little, as she couldn't bear to disentangle herself from him completely. She just needed a little perspective, a moment to cool her head and all the other heated spots she possessed.

"What do you think of the tree?" she whispered.

"Fine."

"You couldn't care less," she said, lifting her chin a fraction.

"Not really."

"Scrooge."

He grinned sinfully. "Bah humbug."

She laughed. "You and this place need some Christmas spirit, Andover."

"What do you have in mind?" he asked, easing his leg farther between her legs, brushing the most intimate part of her with his thigh.

Her pulse throbbing in her ears, she said breathlessly, "Lights, ornaments, maybe a carol or two."

"I don't sing." His hands moved down her body.

"No?"

"No." Pausing at the top of her pants.

Anticipation flowed through her. "Maybe you know how to make music in other ways?"

With a broad grin, he untied her scrubs, eased them down over her hips. "Nurse Roberts, are you coming on to me?"

"Yes, I think so." She wrapped her arms around his neck and captured his mouth—just as he'd captured her heart once so many years before.

Her chin propped on her palm, her leg draped over Clint's thigh, Tara shook her head and smiled at the sad state of affairs they were in. The couch no longer sported its cushions, the coffee table was turned over, its contents strewn about on the floor—all that, and she and Clint were only naked from the waist down.

Frantic and starving for each other, they couldn't be bothered with silly things like getting to the bedroom or undressing fully.

That was for later.

Leaning over, Tara kissed the sharp line of Clint's jaw, then whispered in his ear, "Tell me something that no one knows."

"Hmm, something no one knows." He stretched, his hand caressing her backside. "You have a small strawberry birth mark behind your right ear."

She gave him a playful swat. "Not that kind of something. Something about you that no one knows.

And by the way, that birth mark isn't a total secret—
there are others who know about its existence.''

His expression clouded with mild irritation. ''Who
knows about it?''

She laughed at his apparent jealousy. ''I'll tell you,
but you have to promise not to get any more rankled
than you already are.''

''I don't get rankled,'' he grumbled good-naturedly.
''Now, who's seen it?''

Sighing, she gave up her secret. ''My mother and
my doctor.''

He gave her bottom a playful swat. ''Well, I guess
that's okay.''

''You sound like a possessive lover, you know
that?''

''Well,'' he whispered, nuzzling her neck. ''I
wouldn't mind possessing you again.''

''For tonight?''

The words, the simple query that was not so simple
at all, had slipped out without thought. But perhaps
they were meant to. Perhaps she was asking herself the
question as well as him.

''Tara.'' He pulled her closer, gave her a tender kiss
on the mouth. ''I wish I could offer more—''

''I know,'' she answered for him.

''I want to offer more,'' he clarified, regret evident
in his tone. ''But I can't.''

''Because of the past?'' Why did she have to know?
Why couldn't she just enjoy the time they had together
without questions and hope?

"The only truth is that I have nothing to give anymore. Whether that's due to what happened or..." He inhaled sharply. "Bottom line, you deserve more."

An invisible band squeezed her heart. She didn't agree with his statement. She deserved him, and he her. But obviously, he wasn't ready to recognize that. So for now she would give him what he was ready for. Dipping her head, she gave him a slow, drugging kiss.

He tightened his hold on her. "Tell me something that no one knows, Tara."

"That you're no Scrooge at all," she said, giving him a playful nip on his lower lip. "That you're really a great big teddy bear."

"No." He put a finger under her chin and lifted her gaze to his. "Something about you. Something real."

His need for her to be open and honest with him tore at her soul. He had so much pain hidden behind those eyes. Pain she couldn't even imagine.

Could she draw it out if he gave her, gave them, the time?

Her gaze didn't waver as she looked at him and let her heart bleed, just a little. "Here's something even I didn't know until recently."

"What's that, Tara?"

Emotion swelled within her as she said the words. "I want to love and be loved."

Clint didn't look at all startled. He kissed her tenderly, then lifted her and placed her on his lap. "And I want you."

He began to ease off her top, but Tara stopped him.

Her hand over his, she asked softly, "Let me see you? All of you?"

She felt Clint go rigid, saw his eyes darken danger-ously. "Tara…"

"Please, Clint. I've stood bare before you so many times now, in so many ways. Please."

She watched him struggle for an answer, and her heart hurt for him. But she knew he needed to give in this time.

And when he did, when he released a breath and nodded his head, she smiled.

Straddling him, she took it slowly. As button after button came loose, she prepared herself for what was beneath the black fabric, for what he was so afraid for her to see.

And when she opened his shirt wide, looked down at the pain he had borne for three long years, all she could think was how beautiful he was.

Clint was looking at her, his eyes narrowed, his jaw strained. She knew he expected her to gasp, maybe shriek or shiver at the sight of him, for the craggy, red scar nearly covered the entire left side of his chest.

But she didn't.

She touched him, caressed him. And when she did, he grew hard as granite beneath her.

"One more thing," she said, and eased off her scrub top, unclasped her bra. "I have to feel you against me."

When had she become this wild woman, this hedonist? she wondered as she leaned down and brushed her nipples across his wounded chest.

Clint groaned like an animal, went wild as an animal. He palmed her breasts, then lifting his head, he suckled first one aching bud, then the other, making the wet heat in her womb flow and tease his erection.

She forgot slow. She forgot all. She rose up, found the steel tip of him and sank down. Deep sensation ripped through her, shot into her breasts and made her cry out in pleasure.

He made her so happy, this man she had come to love. A true happiness that would stay with her always. No matter what the outcome of this affair.

Clint gripped her hips as she rode him hard and fast, with no thought or words to dull the pace. She felt stretched and vulnerable and so eager to make him feel again, make him as happy as he made her.

But then his thrusts deepened as he rocked her hips back and forth, setting her mind to fly along with her flesh.

Blinding heat built in her core, and she felt that electric shudder rising to the surface. She wanted to take hold of her pleasure, yet she wanted more of him—this intimacy that was so new and magical.

Trying to hold on to her sanity and to the wants of her unruly body, she dug her fingers into Clint's chest, into that unrelenting burn scar.

"Yes," he muttered, his tone guttural as he locked her hands in place, forcing her to grip him harder.

She lost complete control then—she who had vowed

to never lose control. And when the climax ripped through her, Clint followed, their hips bucking in unison for several seconds afterward until finally she collapsed atop him.

They clung to each other, sweat soaking their bodies. Tara thought of telling him right then and there that she loved him, but quickly decided against it. She would be acting on emotion, not on good sense. And besides that, she knew she couldn't take Clint's reaction if he didn't feel the same.

And odds were he didn't.

Clint rubbed her back, whispered softly in her ear, "I think I should take you to bed now."

"Isn't that what you've been doing for the past several hours?" she replied with a grin.

"I actually mean to sleep this time." He sat up, taking her with him and wrapped his arms around her waist, kissed her hungrily. "You must be exhausted."

She nibbled on his lower lip playfully. "I'm surprisingly awake."

"Are you, now?"

"Yep."

"Well, what are we going to do about that?"

Tara didn't get a chance to find out. From inside of Clint's jacket, his cell phone rang.

He cursed.

"It's okay," she said, easing off his lap.

Regret and annoyance flashed in his eyes. "I'm sorry. My assistant is working on the letter, where the paper came from. I told him to call me if he found out anything.''

''We could use a little break, anyway.'' She smiled. ''I'm going to get some juice. You want some?''

''Thanks.'' He returned her smile as he reached for his phone. ''Hello.''

As she wrapped herself in a blanket and padded into the kitchen, she heard his conversation. Of course it was only one-sided, but she got the gist of it.

''Hey, Ted.''

''This isn't a good time.''

''He was talking about letters?''

Blood pounded in Tara's ears as she poured two glasses of juice. Clint wasn't talking to his assistant. And who was Ted?

''Where is he now?'' Clint asked, his voice grave and subdued.

''I'll be there in ten minutes.''

Tara left the juice on the kitchen counter and headed back into the living room. ''What is it?'' she asked.

''That was my buddy down at the police station. They have a man in custody.'' He was throwing on his clothes. ''Could be the bastard who's been sending the letters. I need to interrogate him.''

''I'll go with you.''

''No.''

''Clint—''

''I want you to stay here. If it is the right guy, I don't want you anywhere near him.'' He pulled on his shoes. "Listen, Ted is sending a squad car over to watch the house, and I'll be back before dawn."

Tara watched him toss on his jacket, her heart aching to make him stay. But that wasn't right. They'd been through so much tonight. He'd trusted her, given her an incredible gift. She would trust him now.

She gave him a quick smile. "Okay."

"Okay? Just like that? No argument?"

"I'm trusting you."

He walked over to her, pulled her into his arms and took her mouth with savage intensity. She returned that kiss with all that she was.

"I'll be back in a few hours," he whispered, then eased away from her and went to the door. "As soon as I'm out the door, you lock up tight, all right?"

She nodded and, when he was gone, did as he asked.

Twelve

The child kissed Tara's cheek, then ran across the fragrant green grass to the swing set. Her blue eyes wide with excitement, the little girl called out for someone.

It was the man sitting beside Tara. A tall, dark, steely-eyed god who made the little girl's mother weak with desire and weaker still with love.

"Daddy, push me," the little girl commanded prettily, her blond curls bouncing about her shoulders as she dropped into one of the swings.

The man beside Tara grinned, then stood up and walked to his daughter. "Anything you say, sweetheart."

They looked so right together, a perfect match.

And as the man pushed the little girl on the swing, up into the blue, where clouds puffed proudly while moving with ease across the sky, Tara wondered what she'd ever done to deserve them.

"Does Mommy want a turn on the swing?" the little girl asked.

"I don't know." The man turned to look in Tara's direction, his blue eyes searching her very soul. "Does she?"

Tara smiled.

She was dreaming. She knew it. But she let the dream continue because in Clint Andover's eyes there was love—a love she'd waited a lifetime to see.

In her dream they had each other and they had their child.

But like all dreams, this one refused to stay.

Tara fought hard to hold on to the image, but it slowly began to fade. Within the confines of her make-believe world, the crystal-blue sky turned bright pink, then orange, then suddenly flaming red.

Tara's pulse began to pound.

Her dream family began to move away as if they were standing on an electric sidewalk. Panic rioted within her and she fought to wake up.

But she didn't seem to have the power or the strength.

She also had no voice, no way to call to her husband and child. She reached for them, but they kept floating backward, frowns upon their beautiful faces.

Crying out, Tara sat bolt upright in bed. But the cry died on her lips and turned into a stuttered choke.

Thick, gray smoke surrounded her.

It took a good five seconds for her to realize what was happening. The house was on fire, the alarm hadn't gone off, and if she didn't get out right now, her dream life would be the only life she would ever know.

Slipping out of bed, she dived for the floor. She'd have to stay low, crawl out of the bedroom and head for the front door.

"Please, God," she begged silently as she scrambled toward the open bedroom door.

But it was no use. The way was blocked, the hallway thick with fire.

Where was Clint? she wondered madly. What time was it? How long had he been gone?

Her throat ached terribly, so dry and scratchy. And her bones felt brittle. But she fought the desperate urge that pooled in her body to lie down, close her eyes and give up.

Turning around, she headed for the bedroom window on shaky arms and wobbly knees. She knew the window was locked, that she'd have to pry open the screen, but it was her only chance.

She felt consumed with fatigue.

She wanted to sleep.

But she was just feet from the window.

Almost there. Almost there.

She could hardly see anymore through the smoke, and her coughing was coming on in spasmodic waves.

Then finally she reached the window. But when she tried to grasp the clamps that held the screen in place, she couldn't. Her muscles didn't seem to be working. Her skin felt too tight, too hot.

And her mind was shutting down.

"Clint…"

On a raspy gasp she collapsed—and the world went dark.

"Passed out cold in his cell." As he walked out of the police station, Clint eyed the cop he'd known since childhood and gave him a frown. "Where did you find that joker?"

Ted Mackay shrugged casually, the lines around his eyes thick with fatigue. "At the bus stop outside the hospital. Looked suspicious—sounded suspicious."

"Well, the location makes sense."

"That's what my officer thought."

Reaching his truck, Clint paused before putting his key in the lock. "Did the guy say anything else?"

Ted shook his head. "Nope. Sorry, buddy. He just babbled on about writing letters to nurses."

"And the officer jumped without asking anything more?"

"He assumed—"

"Wrong assumption."

"Yeah…well, the kid's a rookie, and besides, you know we got to check everything out."

"I know it," Clint stuck out his hand, "and I appreciate you giving me a call."

Ted shook his hand, said, "Hope I didn't interrupt anything but a little sleep." His face split into a wide grin.

An image of Tara, nude, wrapped in a thin sheet flashed into Clint's mind. Pure torture. He sniffed. His friend had interrupted a helluva lot more than sleep.

He'd torn Clint right out of fantasyland.

Clint inhaled deeply. Right now, Tara was probably all warm and soft in her bed. Her arms wrapped around a pillow, her thighs tangled in the sheets.

And here he was, out in the cold—sent away from her on a fool's errand.

Time to get out of here.

Clint gave Ted a wry smile and opened the driver's side door. "Good night, buddy."

"Later, Andover."

He jumped into his truck, but called back, "Let me know if you catch another lead."

"Will do."

Clint gunned the engine, frustration and anticipation building in him at a heady pace. He hadn't felt like this in years, wanting to see a woman so badly, missing her so badly, his body ached. Of course, he wouldn't be admitting that sad fact anytime soon, but it was the truth and it fueled him.

The roads were dark and empty, nothing unusual for four-thirty in the morning. But the silence had him thinking about this case that refused to be solved—and its empty leads.

The idiot had actually passed out twenty minutes after they'd thrown him in the cage. He'd been two beers short of a twelve-pack, and had refused to wake up even when Clint had shaken the hell out of him. But there was his statement, and one of the letters he'd bragged about writing tucked in his jacket pocket.

Both had turned out to be useless. The letters had been nothing more than love letters to half a dozen nurses in Royal Hospital.

Pathetic.

But Clint was satisfied to know that his buddy at the station had his eyes and ears open. Too bad the rookie hadn't found out more information before he'd jumped to conclusions, but hey, mistakes were bound to happen.

He'd get the bastard stalking Jane and Autumn soon enough.

As Clint headed through town, he saw a light on in the bakery and inhaled deeply. Fresh bread, sweet dough, cinnamon. Maybe he should pick up a few rolls for breakfast, surprise Tara with breakfast in bed.

He was about to make a U-turn, when his cell phone rang.

"Andover, here."

"Hey, I hear you were down at the station." Ryan Evans wasn't into any formal hellos. Straight to the point.

Clint could appreciate that. "News travels fast. I'm just leaving there."

"Empty lead, huh?"

"Pretty much."

"Too bad."

Not in the mood to rehash another failed attempt to nab the bastard they were after, Clint changed the subject. "What are you doing up this early?"

"You mean, what am I doing up this late?" The grin in the man's voice was evident.

"Forget I asked," Clint said dryly.

Ryan chuckled. "So, where you headed now? The office?"

"Well, I was going to stop at the bakery. But you sidetracked me."

"The bakery," Ryan drawled with distinct amusement. "Grabbing a little something for you and the beautiful nurse?"

Clint's grip tightened on the steering wheel. "Anything else I can do for you, Evans?"

"Wow."

"I know I'm going to regret saying this, but, 'Wow' what?"

"I never thought I'd see it."

"See what, dammit?"

"Clint Andover, chucking his bachelor status," Ryan replied, disapproval thick in his tone.

"You have no idea what you're talking about," Clint countered icily.

"First Sorrenson, now you. We're falling like leaves. Sad."

As he drove through Tara's neighborhood, he grumbled, "I've got a fist with your name on it, Evans."

Ryan chuckled. "You just name the time and the place, Andover."

The stupid, boyish retort that sat hungrily on his lips faded into the cold, holiday air.

"What the hell?" he uttered, his brow furrowed tightly as he squinted into the distance.

"What's wrong?" Ryan asked, his tone instantly changing from boy to man.

Clint could hardly say the words. They filled him with such dread he nearly stopped the truck.

"There's a fire somewhere."

"Where are you?"

"Close to Tara's. Too close." His voice sounded raw, as though it anticipated something his brain had yet to acknowledge.

But his brain quickly caught up as he rounded the corner.

His heart dropped like a stone.

His curse echoed through the silence.

"Clint?" Ryan shouted through the phone. "Clint, what's going on, man?"

Pulse pounding in his cold blood, Clint let the phone fall from his hand and slammed his foot on the gas. No, it wasn't her place. Couldn't be her place. God wouldn't do this to him again.

He saw a police car a few feet ahead. Ted's man had taken care of her, he thought, grabbing on to an ounce of hope.

But when he came to a screeching halt beside the

car, he found the cop inside passed out—a bloodstain on temple.

Clint took only seconds to jump out of the car and check to see if the officer was still breathing. Then he took off down the road to Tara's place.

Tara's home, which was ablaze with fire.

He'd left her. He'd left her.

And no doubt he would lose her.

As he ran toward the house, his scar pulsing in pain, he heard the screams of a fire truck's siren.

Thirteen

———

Tara could barely breathe.

When she'd come to, a moment ago, she'd thought that perhaps she'd died, that God had taken her before the fire could. But then the heat had gripped her skin, the smoke had flooded her eyes and the fear of what she was up against had raced through her blood, and she knew she was still on earth, still alive.

Still up against the worst nightmare she'd ever known.

As she lay curled up beside the window, she heard the blare of sirens in the distance, but the sound was slightly muffled and held little comfort.

She knew she had to move, to get up, crawl to the

window ledge and open the screen if she wanted to save her life. But though her mind still worked with ideas and solutions, her body refused to respond.

Fear tore at her insides. She didn't want to die; she wasn't ready.

But as the fire crackled, eating away at the flesh of her home, she knew it would come for her soon.

She'd heard of life passing before a person's eyes when they were on the brink of death, and she wondered what she would see when that time came. A lifetime of service? A lifetime of missed opportunities? Of regrets?

Would she see Clint?

A surge of strength moved through her, and she lifted her hand, gripped the wall with her fingernails. It felt hot and she snatched her hand back.

Lord, if she got out of here alive, she would do things differently. Up until now she'd lived her life for others. No balance, no giving to herself. She'd waited to live. But for what?

Again Clint's face drifted into her mind.

If she got out of here alive, she would help them both to accept love.

"Andover, where the hell are you going?"

At first Tara thought the shout had come from outside the window. But it hadn't. It had come from outside the bedroom, in the hall.

"Get the hell out of here!" Tara heard the same voice bellow.

It was the firemen. They were here, trying to get to her without having the whole roof cave in on them all.

But someone didn't seem to care.

"Get out of my way," Clint barked back.

"We're getting to her."

"I'll get to her faster."

"The structure isn't stable."

"I don't give a damn."

"If you don't watch yourself, Andover, you'll get the other half of you charred—"

Clint cursed at them, his voice closer now.

"Clint!" Tara couldn't tell if her cry had any power behind it at all, if it could reach him above the sound of all the chaos and the raging blaze.

"Tara, sweetheart? Where are you?"

"Here," she managed hoarsely. "Here."

She heard him approaching across the floorboards.

"Oh, God, Tara."

Then she felt him beside her, his arm snaking around her waist. She tried to open her eyes, but they weren't working.

"Oh, God, Tara. Hold on."

Her lungs ached and she felt too tired to stay with him.

"Don't fall asleep!"

So tired.

"Don't leave me, dammit. Tara? Can you hear me?"

As she felt herself being lifted, she tried to part her lips, open her mouth, say something, anything to ease the desperation and fear she heard in his voice. He was being destroyed all over again.

Stay awake, she yelled silently. Stay with him. He needed her. He needed to save her. She couldn't have him lose another person he cared about. And she knew he cared for her.

But the effort was too great. Thoughts were slipping. Her body went numb.

Then sooty blackness took her once and for all.

His past had always haunted him.

But over the last three days, it had shown its teeth.

Clint stood in the doorway of Tara's hospital room, staring down at the woman who made his chest tighten with need. She looked so young, so vulnerable—so beautiful.

And so unconscious.

She hadn't woken up once since he'd brought her out of the house three days earlier and placed her on a waiting gurney. Not that he'd expected her to sit up and ask for a glass of water, but as he'd ridden beside her in the ambulance, he'd hoped for a flutter of her eyelids, a sound from her lips. Anything that would tell him she had a good chance of pulling through.

The doctors weren't saying much. A few of them knew him from three years ago and didn't want to raise his hopes this time. But they'd done all they could. It was time to wait and see.

Clint walked to the foot of the bed, a grim expression darkening his face. In contrast, the soft glow of morning sunlight made Tara radiate. Her long, blond curls were splayed about her pillow; her face looked relaxed. Thank God she hadn't suffered any burns, he thought, but the smoke had taken its toll on her throat and lungs.

Raw with fear and needling anxiety, he gripped the edge of the bed to steady himself. If she died he'd never forgive himself.

But if she pulled through, could he actually be forgiving?

"Mr. Andover?"

"Yes." Clint didn't turn around and look at the nurse who'd just entered the room.

"There are a few things I need to do for Tara," she said gently. "Would you mind stepping out for a minute or two."

The thought of leaving her for one moment made him insane, but he wouldn't put up a fight. These were Tara's friends caring for her, giving her their best, and he had to trust their judgment.

Clint walked blindly from the room, then down the hall to the waiting area. David Sorrenson was at his ranch, guarding Jane and Autumn. But Ryan and Alex were there, silent, pretending to read the newspaper. They eased to their feet when they saw him.

"How you holding up?" Ryan asked.

Clint shook his head. "I'm not."

Giving his friend an understanding nod, he said, "Any word on her condition?"

"No."

"Anything we can do..."

"You can bring me that bastard's head on a platter," Clint ground out, his hands balling into fists at his sides.

"Done," the men said in unison.

Maybe it was an empty promise, for they had no clue who the man was, but their impassioned pledge was good to hear. Just as their company was good to have.

Something else that had changed since he'd known Tara. He was willing to accept help from his buddies at the TCC instead of having to do it all, protect it all, himself.

Through her, he'd realized that it wasn't a weakness to need someone—it was weakness to pretend that you needed no one.

"Have you heard anything from the police or the fire department?" Clint asked.

"They're pretty sure it was arson."

"What a surprise," Clint muttered sarcastically. "If Tara…if she… Well, let's just say that bastard doesn't want me to be the one who catches him."

Ryan cuffed him on the shoulder. "You should go home, man, get some sleep."

Clint shook his head. "I'm not going anywhere. Not yet."

Alex turned to Ryan, gave him a frown. "You don't leave the woman you love, idiot."

"Did you just call me an idiot?"

"Yes, I believe I did."

Ryan's eyes narrowed. "Good thing we're in a hospital. When I finish with you, they won't have to take you far.''

Clint barely heard the boys-will-be-boys argument. His anger had dropped away, while his mind had stopped on one word, one thought.

Love.

The word stabbed at his heart, just as Tara had unknowingly done a hundred times before, trying to break through his iron will by being the amazing, caring and provocative woman that she was.

Love.

Was it possible? Had a feeling like that penetrated his scarred chest? Found its way into a man who truly believed he could never love another woman in his life? Or that he deserved to love another?

His mouth tight and grim, he knifed his hands through his hair. He'd never thought it possible, but this was Tara...

"Look at him," Ryan said, now bored of trading insults with Alex. "He's so out of it. I think he needs some sleep."

"What I need is her," Clint said tightly.

Ryan nodded.

Alex gave him a pat on the back. "We're here for you."

He gave them both a nod of thanks, then said, "I'm going back in," and walked out of the waiting room.

He needed to get to Tara. Even if she couldn't hear him, he had to tell her how she'd changed him, how her spirit and care had made his nightmares go away.

He needed to hold her in his arms and tell her that she'd eased him out of his past.

And made him want to live again.

The confusing world of her hospital room came into focus in a slow, complicated way. Like a newborn baby opening her eyes for the very first time, Tara saw light, then recognized object, then movement.

And finally the man who sat beside her bed.

"Clint?" she said, her voice raw, hoarse, still caked with smoke.

He nodded, his gaze all tenderness. "Thank God. I could only hope you'd come back to me."

He sounded far away, but she knew better. She knew she wasn't dreaming. She knew this wasn't heaven.

Or was it?

Tara struggled to keep her gaze on him, but her eyelids felt heavy. She blinked a few times. Looking far too handsome than any man had a right in a black sweater and jeans, Clint Andover—dream man of her child- and adulthood—smiled down at her. "Merry Christmas, sweetheart."

Her brain felt a bit muddled. Had she been unconscious that long…? "It's Christmas?"

"Christmas Eve. But I feel like celebrating early." He lifted a brow. "You don't mind do you?"

She managed a small smile. "Not at all."

"Got to say, though, having you awake is one helluva present, Nurse Roberts."

The way he looked at her, as though he truly cherished her—it was how she'd always imagined it would be.

"How long have I been asleep?" she asked him then. "If it's Christmas Eve—"

Deep regret flashed in his eyes. "It's been a few days."

At that news Tara let her head fall back against the pillow. A few days. She closed her eyes, allowed the memory of smoke and fire and fear rush up on her like an ocean wave. She'd had a terrifying experience, one she would remember forever.

But it was over, she reminded herself, letting her lids rise, letting her gaze find Clint's once again, and she could cling to that.

And to the look in this man's eyes right now.

If she didn't know better, she would swear it was the look of—

She mentally shook off that thought and asked softly, "It was him, wasn't it?"

"We think so."

"Why? I wish I understood."

"No sane person can understand the actions of the *in*sane, Tara."

A shiver drifted up her spine, weakened her a little more. "Jane and the baby—"

"Are fine," Clint assured her.

"My house—"

"Don't think about it."

"My house?" she said again, this time with more force than she thought was in her. She knew the answer, or suspected it at any rate. But she needed to hear him say it.

He took a deep breath, released it, then shook his head. "I'm sorry."

Tara turned away, her heart paining her profoundly. It was her family home. The place where she'd grown up, loved and cared for her mother. And later, it had been her respite from the world and from the woman she had to be when she was outside of its walls.

And lately, the place where she'd stripped her most basic self and allowed the woman she had always wanted to be out.

It had been in that house that she'd defied her own limitations and fallen in love.

Taking her hand in his, Clint brought it to his lips. "But you're here. You're alive."

"Yes."

He bent toward her. "And whether you accept it or not, you have a home. With me."

"What?"

"That is, if you can ever forgive me." His voice was tight, strained.

"For what?"

"Leaving you that night—"

"That fire wasn't your fault," she said with all the passion she could muster. "Neither fire was your fault. You must realize that. You are nothing but a wonderful, caring man. And a great protector."

His jaw tight, his eyes glistening with unshed tears, Clint said, "I love you so much, Tara."

Tara felt stunned. She hadn't heard him correctly. "You do?"

"Desperately," he told her. Leaning in, he gave her a tender kiss.

"Clint…"

His forehead to hers, his voice filled with emotion, he said, "I never thought I could care for someone again. I thought I was dead. Hell, I think I was." He sat up, took her hand and placed it on his chest. "This scar was me, sweetheart. Burned, wrecked, maybe healing a little, but in a damaged way."

Tara couldn't believe her ears. If it weren't that she was feeling the ache of a night racked by fire and smoke and terror, and three days of recovery in bed, she'd swear she was lost in a dream. That beautiful dream. The one where Clint's and her child came running in and leaped up beside them on the bed.

But this was real.

Clint gazed down at her with loving, desperate eyes. "These past several weeks have been the most amazing, surprising and perfect weeks I've known in a long time." He shook his head. "Who would have ever thought… I mean, we were brought together under the most bizarre of circumstances."

"Terrifying."

"Yes, but—"

"But?" she said, her pulse tapping a little faster in her blood.

"I never thought I'd say this, but out of adversity came this. This amazing love."

"You really love me?" she asked, needing to hear his reassurance over and over again.

"You have no idea how much."

"Oh, Clint, I..."

I love you, too.

She stopped cold.

What was wrong with her? Tara wondered, feeling completely overwhelmed by the moment. She'd been in love with this man forever it seemed, and had admitted it to herself weeks ago, but now... Why couldn't she say the words?

A chuckle eased from Clint's throat. "Don't be afraid to say it, sweetheart. It doesn't hurt as much as I thought it would."

"Hurt?"

"The pain of letting all your control, all your self-protective instincts go right out the window—it's a scary prospect."

Tara just stared at him, amazed at who he'd become, who she'd always known he was.

He smiled at her. "Saying what you feel and asking for what you want. It feels pretty darn good."

She wanted to. So badly, she wanted to. For too many years she'd bottled her feelings like an aging wine in a dusty cellar. She'd had to, to survive, care for herself and others. It had been her sacrifice.

She gazed up at Clint, saw the truth in his eyes, saw her future, what she could have if she was brave enough to accept it.

"I love you, too," she said, hoisting herself up a

few inches, wanting to be at his level, a real player in this glorious game. "So much I ache with it."

He moved closer, the heat from his body radiating into her. "Can we start our lives over, Tara?"

"Together?"

"Yes."

"With promises and a house of our own and—"

"Babies?" she said quickly.

His smile widened. "Lots of babies."

Tara's mouth trembled, and she swallowed the lump in her throat. "Oh, yes."

"Marry me?"

"When?" Her heart seemed to stand still.

He chuckled. "As soon as possible."

"Sooner," she said on a laugh, then slowed when she started coughing. "Well, maybe we should give it a few days. Just until I'm well enough to leave the hospital."

He kissed her tenderly again, then turned around and lay down beside her on the hospital bed. "That sounds like the perfect plan," he said as he put his arms around her and held her close.

Tara closed her eyes for a moment, sending up a silent prayer of gratitude.

"Thank you," she whispered against Clint's chest.

"For what, sweetheart."

"For rescuing me."

"From the fire?" he asked, pulling her closer.

With a soft smile playing about her lips, Tara buried her head in his chest. "From the fire, yes. But more important, from a life without you."

Epilogue

Five days later...

The wedding took place under the white arch of the gazebo where they'd shared their first kiss, their second kiss and, tonight, the kiss that had made them husband and wife.

Clint Andover took the hand of his beautiful bride and led her down the steps and down the red velvet aisle that ran between the two hundred guests in attendance.

A hoot went up amongst the crowd, and the guests all jumped to their feet in one minute of uninterrupted thunderous applause.

Grinning from ear to ear, Clint straightened his shoulders, stood a little taller. This was a day he'd never thought he would see again. But Tara had changed him, changed his life, and he knew that with her by his side his past could finally rest, along with the nightmares that used to plague him.

Around them the celebration got under way with music and merriment, food and drink. Clint led Tara into the reception area, dressed up just as she'd planned. Under a starry Texas sky, surrounded by trees and perfectly placed heaters, a serving staff milled about with trays of champagne and spiced rum punch, cheese puffs and caviar on toast. It was elegant and earthy at the same time.

He grinned at his wife. Just as she was.

"Mind if we steal your bride for a minute?" Marissa Sorrenson, with a slightly somber Jane Doe at her side, gave him an eager look.

Clint nodded, but added with mock severity, "Only for a few minutes, though. Then she's all mine."

Marissa grinned at the romance of it all, and she and Jane led Tara away. Which in turn left Clint at the mercy of his TCC brothers, who had a few choice words for him.

"I can't believe that you and Sorrenson actually took the plunge," Ryan said, shaking his head with regret. "What the hell is happening around here?"

Chuckling, David slapped his friend on the back. "You could be next, Evans."

"Get serious."

"What about you, Kent?"

Alex snorted. "It's going to take more than a pretty face to get me into another one of these monkey suits, I can promise you that."

"When the right woman comes along..." Clint said ominously.

"That's the trouble." Ryan grinned broadly. "Too many right women, too little time."

Alex nodded, grabbing a glass of champagne. "Sounds about right."

"Well, boys, happy hunting. I have a date to dance with my very right woman." David chuckled and moved off in Marissa's direction.

Clint thrust his full glass of champagne into Alex's hand. "I second that."

The two men chuckled but called out their congratulations as Clint made his way over to Tara. He found her near the dance floor, still talking with Marissa and Jane.

For just a moment he took her in. She looked like an angel in her winter-white bridal gown, her blond curls falling loose about her shoulders, her eyes bright and her cheeks pink with cold—or maybe they were glowing with love.

"May I have this dance, Mrs. Andover?" he asked, sidling up beside her, bowing at the waist.

On a pretty laugh, she curtsied and replied, "I would be delighted, Mr. Andover."

Under the watchful gaze of Marissa, Jane and David,

and maybe a few hundred others, he led Tara out onto the makeshift dance floor.

"Did I tell you how beautiful you look tonight?" he asked, taking her in his arms and holding her close as the music played and the guests talked and laughed and celebrated under the brilliant holiday moon.

"Yes, you did," she said, her voice soft and husky. "But I love hearing it again."

"Then I'll keep saying it."

Tara rose on her toes, gave him a teasing kiss, then said breathlessly, "And I'll keep plying you with kisses when you do."

"I'm going to hold you to that," he said, pulling her impossibly closer.

"Oh, I hope so." She grinned. "Hey, we didn't make a toast to our guests."

"How about a few private ones instead?"

"Perfect."

He kissed her softly. "Here's to the coming New Year."

"Absolutely."

Again his mouth closed over hers. "And here's to life."

"And to love," she whispered.

He grinned. "To past and future."

"To kids and old age."

His chest tight with emotion, Clint stopped in the middle of the floor, in the middle of the song, and cupped her face in his hands. "To you, my sweet Tara."

As she looked up into his eyes, the love he saw there was bright and irresistible, but it was the words she uttered next that truly healed his wounded soul.

"And to you, my love."

*   *   *   *   *

Don't miss the next installment of the
TEXAS CATTLEMAN'S CLUB:
THE STOLEN BABY!

*Meet Travis Whelan—a jet-setting
attorney...and a* father?
*When Natalie Perez showed up
in his life again with the baby daughter
he hadn't known about,
Travis knew he had a duty
to both of them.
But could he find a way
to make them a family?*

REMEMBERING ONE WILD NIGHT
by Kathie DeNosky
*Coming to you from Silhouette Desire
in January 2004.*

*And now for a sneak preview of
REMEMBERING ONE WILD NIGHT,
please turn the page.*

One

When Jane heard the doorbell chime, she anxiously glanced around the room full of happy people. This might be the opportunity she'd been waiting for. Everyone's attention seemed to be directed toward the two men who had just arrived for David and Marissa Sorrenson's New Year's Eve party.

Rising to her feet, she turned and walked calmly but purposefully down the hall. She didn't want to see who the late arrivals were. It didn't matter. She wouldn't know them anyway.

Jane sighed heavily. She didn't even know who she was, and since she'd been unable to remember much about herself in the past couple of months, it was beginning to look as if she never would.

But whatever her name was, it was clear that she was putting those around her in danger. Some of them had already received threatening letters, and Tara had even lost her home because Jane had been staying with her.

Jane would always be grateful for their kindness and generosity, but she refused to jeopardize their safety any longer. That's why she'd come to the agonizing decision that it was time for her and her baby daughter, Autumn, to leave Royal, Texas.

Entering the room she'd been sharing with the baby since Tara's house had been destroyed by an arsonist, Jane quickly wrote a note thanking everyone for their help. Then, gathering her daughter's things, she placed them in a bag, put her jacket on and wrapped the baby in a warm blanket. Careful not to wake Autumn, Jane picked her up and walked quickly down the hall.

She'd take the back way to the kitchen to avoid being seen, get a couple of bottles of formula from the refrigerator, then slip out the back door undetected. With any luck, she'd be well on her way before anyone noticed they were missing or found the note explaining why she'd made the decision to leave.

Once she had the baby bottles tucked inside the new diaper bag Marissa had given her, she started for the door. But just as she put her hand on the polished brass knob, a male voice stopped her in her tracks.

"Jane, I've got a couple more Club members that

I'd like you to meet,'' Ry Evans announced from behind her. ''Hey, where are you going?''

She heard the confusion in his voice, and, slowly
turning to face him, Jane tried to think of an excuse
for why she would be taking the baby outside at such
a late hour. ''I thought I would—''

Noticing the man standing beside Ry, she stopped
short. There was something very familiar about him.
About an inch shorter than Ry's six-foot height, he had
short, light brown hair, hazel eyes and...

''Natalie,'' the man said incredulously, taking a step
toward her.

She opened her mouth to ask him why he'd called
her by that name, but with sudden, blinding clarity she
knew. Her name was Natalie—Natalie Perez. She was
twenty-five years old and lived in Chicago.

Blinking, she watched the handsome man take a step
toward her. His name was Travis Whelan. He was
thirty-two, a millionaire and...

Her head began to throb as realization slammed into
her with the force of a physical blow. He wasn't just
someone she'd once known.

Travis Whelan was her baby's father, and the man
she'd sworn she'd never wanted to see again.

You are about to enter the exclusive,
masculine world of the...

The Stolen Baby

Silhouette Desire's powerful miniseries features
six wealthy Texas bachelors—all members of the
state's most prestigious club—who must unravel
the mystery surrounding one tiny baby...and
discover true love in the process!

ENTANGLED WITH A TEXAN by Sara Orwig
(Silhouette Desire #1547, November 2003)

LOCKED UP WITH A LAWMAN by Laura Wright
(Silhouette Desire #1553, December 2003)

REMEMBERING ONE WILD NIGHT by Kathie DeNosky
(Silhouette Desire #1559, January 2004)

BREATHLESS FOR THE BACHELOR by Cindy Gerard
(Silhouette Desire #1564, February 2004)

PRETENDING WITH THE PLAYBOY by Cathleen Galitz
(Silhouette Desire #1569, March 2004)

FIT FOR A SHEIKH by Kristi Gold
(Silhouette Desire #1576, April 2004)

Available at your favorite retail outlet.

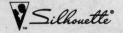

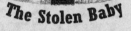

eHARLEQUIN.com

For **FREE online reading,** visit
www.eHarlequin.com now and enjoy:

Online Reads
Read **Daily** and **Weekly** chapters from
our Internet-exclusive stories by your
favorite authors.

Red-Hot Reads
Turn up the heat with one of our more
sensual online stories!

Interactive Novels
Cast your vote to help decide how these
stories unfold…then stay tuned!

Quick Reads
For shorter romantic reads, try our
collection of Poems, Toasts, & More!

Online Read Library
Miss one of our online reads?
Come here to catch up!

Reading Groups
Discuss, share and rave with other
community members!

For great reading online,
visit www.eHarlequin.com today!

Silhouette®

Desire ®

January 2004

A brand-new
family saga begins.

DYNASTIES : THE DANFORTHS

A family of prominence...
tested by scandal,
sustained by passion!

Become immersed in the lives of
the Danforths and enter the
high-powered world of Savannah society.
Danforth patriarch Abraham Danforth's
surprising decision to run for state Senate
will unleash a chain of events uncovering
long-hidden secrets, testing this family
more than they ever imagined.

Available at your favorite retail outlet.

COMING NEXT MONTH